M.Y.T.H. Inc. In Action

M.Y.T.H. Inc.
In Action

by
Robert L. Asprin

Cover and Interior Art
by Phil Foglio

Edited by Beverley Hainer

Starblaze Editions
The Donning Company/Publishers
Norfolk/Virginia Beach

Other titles in this series:

Another Fine Myth
Myth Conceptions
Myth Directions
Hit or Myth
Myth-ing Persons
Little Myth Marker
M.Y.T.H. Inc. Link
Myth-Nomers and Im-Pervections

Graphic novels

Myth Adventures One (with Phil Foglio)
Myth Adventures Two (with Phil Foglio)

For information on how to join the Myth Adventures Fan Club, write to Myth Adventures, P.O. Box 95, Sutter, CA 95982-0095.

Copyright © 1990 by Robert L. Asprin
Cover and illustrations copyright © 1990 by Phil Foglio

The Donning Company/Publishers
5659 Virginia Beach Boulevard
Norfolk, Virginia 23502

Library of Congress Cataloging-in-Publication Data:

Asprin, Robert.
    M.Y.T.H. Inc. in action / by Robert Asprin; edited by Beverley Hainer; cover and interior art by Phil Foglio.
        p. cm. --(Ninth book of Myth Adventure series)
Library of Congress Number: 90-082207
ISBN: 0-89865-788-1 (ltd.):$40.95 --ISBN: 0-89865-787-3 (pbk.): $8.95
    I. Hainer, Beverley. II. Title. III. Series: Asprin, Robert. Myth Adventure series; 9th bk.
PN3551.S6M16 1990
741.5'973--dc20   90-3376
                                              CIP

Dedication

*With affection and apologies to my
many foreign translators
...especially those at my German publisher,
Bastei Lubbe!*

Author's Note

I am not a fast writer,
I am not a slow writer,
I am a half fast writer!
R.L. Asprin

The fan mail I've received has been pretty much split on the subject of my last Introduction; some found it interesting and insightful, while others thought it was boring and a waste. If you are of the latter group, please feel free to jump ahead directly into the story, since there is nothing in this message you need to know to understand (and, hopefully, enjoy) the book.

For the rest of you, this note is mostly an apology... or, more accurately, a string of apologies.

Back in *M.Y.T.H. Inc. Link*, I optimistically stated that I would be trying to write two Myth episodes a year... and things have not been the same since. I, my publishers, and many bookstores and dealers have been flooded with queries and demands for "the next Myth book," with each reader being *sure* the books were in existence somewhere because of the schedule I had so foolishly "committed to" in that introduction.

To belabor the obvious, I haven't been able to write at the speed I anticipated at the time. While the popularity of the series and the loyalty of its readers is both gratifying and profitable, any publisher can tell you that trying to get a book out of an author when "it isn't happening" is like pushing on a rope. You see, when I made my writing "guesstimate," I had just finished writing *MIL*, and the speed with which the prose goes onto the page when I'm closing on the end of a book was still fresh in my mind. That is, when it's flowing, it flows very fast. What I had overlooked was the months of outlining and false starts that go on *before* things get flowing. (These books only *look* spontaneous and easy to write. Honest!) Anyway, the cruel realities of the situation surfaced when I tried to meet my promised schedule, and I fell far behind my anticipated timetable. As the queries and demands from the readers grew, the tolerance of the publishers for late delivery grew less and less, and the pressures on me increased "to get the manuscript in" with less and less time for rewrites and polish.

Finally, in 1988, things blew up. I got into a dispute with Donning/Starblaze (the prime Myth publisher... the mass market [small paperback] editions from Ace are subcontracted reprints) over royalties. The dispute has been settled, and the only reason I mention it here is that it lasted the better part of a year... delaying my writing that much more.

In addition to the negotiated terms of that settlement, however, there is an additional apology that I owe the management of Donning. You see, part of the settlement was that the next book (the one you're holding) would not be advertised nor orders taken until the manuscript had been delivered. This was an effort to take some of the "deadline" pressure off my writing as I tried to get back into stride. There were two unfortunate side effects of that condition, however. First, I was unable to reply to the many readers and fans asking when the next book would be out... as it would be less than fair to insist that Donning not advertise a release date, then banter it about myself. Secondly, at one point I gave my assurance to Donning on the phone as to when the manuscript would be completed... then promptly forgot that I had done so. This meant that when I encountered problems with my writing, I neglected to warn Donning of the delay, and in that absence of revised information, they launched an extensive and expensive advertising campaign for the release of the book in late '89... only to suffer embarrassment and loss of credibility when the manuscript failed to appear for production.

While I am not in a position to repair the financial damage caused by the "false start" advertising campaign, I feel it only honorable to offer public apology to Donning for the professional embarrassment which my memory lapse caused. For the record, the late appearance of this volume is due to delays at the author's end, not the publisher, distributor, bookstore, or dealer. Writers are often quite loud in voicing horror stories about having their works mishandled by the publishing industry, yet not so vocal when it comes to admitting their own shortcomings. Folks, this time the confusion and delays were **my fault**, and the distress I feel because of that will only be compounded if I allow others to take the blame by remaining silent.

While I'm prattling, let me try to head off another potential round of misunderstanding and confusion. In July of '90, another humor series of mine, science fiction this time, will premiere with the publishing of *Phule's Company*. Please do not panic. This new series is *in addition to, not replacing,* the MYTH novels. As promised back in *MIL*, the MYTH novels will continue *at least* through #12.

(More than) Enough said. While this intro hasn't been as much fun as the last, look at it as a different sort of insight into the "carefree life of an author" and the frustrating complexities of the publishing industry. Enjoy the book. I only hope it justifies the wait.

Robert Lynn Asprin
February 1990

Introduction

"What am I doing here?"
Any recruit, any army

Name?"

Now, in those circles within whose company I am accustomed to travelin', it is considered impolite to ask questions in general... and that question in specific. Unfortunately, I was currently well outside those circles, and as such felt compelled to answer the inquiry, however rude.

"Guido."

"Home address?"

"The Bazaar at Deva."

"What?"

"The Bazaar at...Oh! Uh...just say...'varies.'"

The joker what was takin' down this information gives me a hard look before continuing with his questions. I give him my best innocent look back, which as any jury can tell you is most convincin', though deep down inside I am more than a little annoyed with myself. Bein' a smarter than average individual, I should have recalled that even though my travels and adventures with the Boss have accustomed me to other dimensions, to most folks here on Klah such places as the Bazaar at Deva are unheard of, and therefore suspicious. As I am makin' a specific effort to be inconspicuous, this is not the wisest answer to have given.

"Height and weight?"

This question makes me feel a bit better, as it serves to remind me that whatever I say or do, I will never be totally inconspicuous. You see, I am what is politely referred to as "a large person"...or less politely as "a knuckle-dragging monster." While this is of invaluable assistance considerin' my chosen profession, it does, however, make it difficult to blend with any given crowd. In fact, I would be the largest person in the line if it were not for Nunzio who is maybe an inch shorter, but a bit bulkier.

I can see the guy with the questions has noticed this all by himself, since he keeps glancin' back and forth between the two of us as he jots down my responses.

"Next of kin?"

"I guess that would be Nunzio, here," I sez, jerkin' a thumb at my colleague.

"You two are related?"

"He's my cousin."

"Oh."

For a second I think he's about to say somethin' more, but then he just shrugs and scribbles a little more on his pad.

"Do you have a criminal record?"

"Beg pardon?"

"A criminal record. Have you ever been arrested?"

"No convictions."

That earns me another hard look.

"I didn't ask about convictions. I asked if you've ever been arrested."

"Well...yeah. Hasn't everybody?"

"What for?"

"Which time?"

"How many times have you been arrested?"

"Oh, three...maybe four dozen times...but no convictions."

The joker has his eyebrows up now.

"You've been arrested nearly fifty times with no convictions?"

"No witnesses," I say, showin' him my teeth.

"I see," the guy sez, lookin' a little nervous, which is one of the customary side effects of my smiles. "Well...let's try it this way...are you currently wanted by the authorities?"

"No."

"Good...good," he nods, fillin' in that blank on the form in front of him.

"Okay...one final question. Do you know of any reason why you should not be allowed to enlist in the army of Possiltum?"

In the actualities of the situational, I knew of *several* reasons not to enlist...startin' with the fact that I didn't want to and endin' with the godawful wardrobe that I would be forced to wear as a soldier-type.

"Naw."

"Very well," he sez, pushin' the form across the table at me. "Just sign or make your mark here, please."

"Is that all?" I ask, scribblin' my name in the indicated spot.

"Is that all, *sergeant*," the joker smiles, pickin' up the paper and blowin' on the signature.

Another reason for not joinin' the army occurs to me.

"Is that all, *sergeant*? I sez, bein' careful not to let my annoyance show.

"No. Go to the next tent now and you'll be issued a uniform. Then report back here and you'll be assigned to a group for your training."

"Training?"

This is indeed somethin' what had never occurred to me or Nunzio, and could put a serious crimp in our projected timetable. I mean, how much trainin' does it take to kill people?"

"That's right... training," the sergeant sez with a tight-lipped smile.

"There's more to being a soldier than wearing a uniform, you know."

Bein' a survival oriented individual, I refrain from speculatin' out loud as to what this might entail. Fortunately, the sergeant does not seem to expect an answer or additional comment. Rather, he waves me out the door as he turns his attention to the next unfortunate.

"Name?"

"Nunzio."

Now, those of youse what have been followin' dese books all along may be wonderin' just why it is that Nunzio and me is signin' onto Possiltum's army instead of performin' our normal duties of bodyguardin' the Boss... who you probably think of as the Great Skeeve, as you is not employed by him and therefore

14

have no reason to think of him as the Boss.

This confusion is understandable, as this book is happenin' right after the book before the last one. (*M.Y.T.H. Inc. Link*) and at the same time as the one before this (*Myth-Nomers and Im-Pervections*). Add to that the fact that this is one of the M.Y.T.H. Inc. volumes, and is therefore bein' told from my viewpoint instead of the Boss's, and it becomes clear why your eyes is perhaps crossed at this point in the narrative. The only consolin' I can offer youse, is that if youse think my life whilst workin' for the Boss is confusin' to read, youse should try *livin'* it for a month or five!

Actually, to be totally honest with youse, dis book is not startin' where I was the last time you saw me, so let me refer youse back to the meetin' which started us on this particular chain of events...

Chapter 1

*"What do you mean
my characters talk funny?"*
D. Runyon

It is indeed a privilege to be included in a war-type council, regardless of what war it is or who in specific is also attendin'. Only the very elite are involved, which is to say those who will be furthest from the actual fightin', as such gatherin's are usually concerned with which portions of one's forces are expendable, and exactly how and when they are to be expended. Since it is demoralizin' for those who are to be dropped into the meat grinder to know they have been chosen as "designated receivers," they are logically excluded from the proceedin's, seein' as how if they are made aware of their roles in advance, they are apt to take it on the lam rather than dutifully expiring on schedule, thereby botchin' up many hours of plannin' on both sides of the dispute

16

in question. From this, it is easy to see that attendin' these borin' but necessary plannin' sessions is not only an honor, it greatly improves one's chances of bein' alive at the end of the fracas. To get killed in a battle one has had a hand in settin' the strategies for is an indication that one's plannin' abilities are sorely lackin' and will count heavily against youse when bein' considered for future engagements.

In this particular circumstantial, however, it was no special honor to be included in the plannin' session, as our entire force consisted of a mere five personages... six if you count the Boss's dragon. Needless to say, none of us was inclined to think of ourselves as fallin' into the "expendable" category. Realizin', however, that we was supposed to be trying to stop a renegade queen with a sizable mob of army-types at her disposal, one was not inclined to make book on our chances for survival... unless, of course, one was offered irresistible odds and maybe a decent point spread.

While there wasn't all that many of us, I, for one, had no complaints with the quality of our troops.

Tananda and Chumley are a sister and brother, Trollop and Troll team. While they are some of the nicest people it has ever been my pleasure to encounter, either of them is also as capable as any five knee-breakers ever employed by the Mob if they find it necessary to be unpleasant. In the Boss's absence, they have taken it on themselves to be the leaders of our expedition...an arrangement which suits me fine.

You see, my cousin Nunzio and me is far more comfortable takin' orders than givin' them. This is a habit we have acquired workin' for the Mob, where the less you know about why an order is bein' givin', the better off you are...particularly if at a later point you should be called upon to explain your actions under oath. (For those of youse who have failed to read about our activities in the earlier books in this series and are therefore ignorant as to our identities and *modus operandi,* our job description refers to us as "collection specialists"... which is a polite way of sayin' we're kneecappers.)

The fifth member of our little strike force is Massha... and if that name alone is not sufficient to summon forth an identifyin' image in your mind, then it is obvious you have not yet met this particular individual in the flesh. You see, Massha has a singularly unique appearance which is unlikely to be mistaken for anyone else, though she might, perhaps, be mistaken for some-*thing* else...like maybe a dinosaurous if said saurous was bein' used as a travelin' display for a make-up and jewelry trade show. What I am tryin' to say is that Massha is both very big and very colorful, but in the interest of brevity I will spare you the analogous type comparisons. What is important is that as big and as tough as she is, Massha has a heart even bigger than her dress size.

We had been holdin' the start of our meetin' until she got back from droppin' the Boss off on Perv, which she had just done, so now we are ready to commence the proceedin's.

"So you're tellin' me you think King Rodrick was whacked by Queen Hemlock? That's why Skeeve sent you all here?"

18

This is Big Julie talkin'. While me and Nunzio have never met this particular individual before, we have heard of his reputation from the days when he also worked for the Mob, and it seems he and the Boss are old friends and that he's one of our main sources for information and advice in this dimension. In any case, we are usin' his villa as a combination meetin' point and base of operations for this caper.

"That's right," Tananda sez. "Hemlock's always been big on world conquest, and it looks like her new husband wouldn't go along with her schemes."

"Realizing she now has the combined power of her kingdoms' money and the military might of your old army," Chumley adds, "It occurred to Skeeve that she might be tempted to try to... shall we say, expand her holdings a bit. Anyway, he asked us to pop over and see first hand what was happening."

"I see," Big Julie nods, sippin' thoughtfully at his wine. "To tell you the truth, it never occurred to me that the king's dyin' was a little too convenient to be accidental. I'm a little surprised, though, that Skeeve isn't checkin' this out himself. Nothin' personal, but he never used to be too good at delegatin'."

"He's busy," Massha sez, cuttin' it short like a casino pit boss.

Tananda shoots her a look then leans forward, puttin' a comfortin' hand on her knee.

"He'll be all right, Massha. Really."

Massha makes a face, then heaves one of her big sighs.

"I know. I'd just feel a lot better if he let a couple of us tag along, is all. I mean, that *is*

Perv he's wandering around in. They've never been noted for their hospitality."

"Perv?" Big Julie scowls. "Isn't that where that weirdo Aahz is from?"

"Where he's from, and where he's gone," Chumley supplies. "He and Skeeve had a falling out, and friend Aahz has quit the team. Skeeve has gone after him to try to bring him back... which leaves us to deal with Queen Hemlock. So tell us, Jules, what's the old girl been up to lately?"

"Well, I'll admit there's been a lot of activity since the king died," Julie admits. "The army's been on the move almost constantly, and both they and the kingdom are getting noticeably bigger... know what I mean? It's kinda like the old days when I was running the army, only on a bigger scale. I get a post card from one of the boys sayin' how they're visitin' a new country, than ga-bing-ga-bang that country's suddenly a new part of Possiltum."

"I see," the troll sez thoughtfully. "Well, what do you think, little sister? You're the only one here who was along the last time Skeeve stopped this particular army."

"Not quite. You're forgetting that Gleep was there... and, of course, Big Julie."

She winks at that notable who responds with a gracious half bow. Gleep, the Boss's dragon, raises his head and looks around at the mention of his name, then sighs and goes back to sleep.

"'Course, I was on the other side last time," Big Julie sez, "but it occurs to me that you got your work cut out for you this time around."

"How so?"

"Well, last time we was the invaders, you

know? The locals didn't like us, even though they didn't take much of a hand in the resistance Skeeve organized. This time, though, the army is the home team, and folks in the kingdom are pretty much behind 'em all the way."

"You mean the kingdomers are in favor of the queen's new expansion moves?" Tananda frowns.

"That's right," Big Julie nods, "and when you think about it, it stands to reason. The bigger the kingdom gets, the more people there are to share the cost, so the taxes get smaller. With their taxes goin' down with each new conquest, the citizens are positively ecstatic about the way things are going. If that weren't enough, unemployment is at an all time low what with so many goin' into the army, so pay scales are sky high."

"So Hemlock's running a popular war, eh?" Tananda sez, pursing her lips thoughtfully. "Maybe that's the route for us to go. What do you think, big brother?"

This last she directs at Chumley, who just shrugs.

"I suppose it's as good a place as any to start. Something about that analysis of the tax structure bothers me, though."

I tended to agree with Chumley, but Tananda is on a roll.

"Save it for the financial heavyweights," she waves. "For the time being, let's focus on doing what we're good at."

"And just what do you figure that is?" Massha interrupts. "Excuse me, but could you two run that by again slowly for the benefit of those of us who aren't used to your brother/ sister shorthand?"

"Well, the way I see it, our best bet is to work on making Hemlock's expansion program unpopular. I mean, there's not much the five of us can do about stopping the army by ourselves, but if we can get the populace worked up maybe the queen will have to reconsider... or at least slow down."

"We could try to kill her," Massha sez pointedly.

"True," Tananda acknowledges, "and don't think I haven't given that option some serious thought. I think it's a little more drastic than Skeeve had in mind when he sent us on this mission, though. Anyway, I think I'd like to hold that option in reserve for now, or at least until Skeeve catches up with us and we have a chance to clear it with him."

"Well, if you don't mind, there's another possibility I'd like to try."

"What's that, Massha?"

"Tell me, Big Julie, is General Badaxe still running the army?"

"Hugh?" Sure is. He's a fast learner, that one. Remembers mostly everything I've taught him about runnin' an army."

"Well," Massha sez, heaving herself to her feet," I think I'll just wander off and try to find his headquarters. He had quite a thing for me the last time I was through. Maybe if I look him up again, I can get his mind off running the army for a while, or at least distract him enough that they won't be quite so efficient."

"I say, that's a good idea, Massha," Chumley sez. "Speaking of the army, Guido, do you think you and Nunzio can manage to sign up for a hitch? Remembering how you stirred things up at the Acme magik factory by getting the workers to unionize, you're the logical choice for demoralizing the troops, and that's best done from the inside."

"Yea, sure," I sez with a shrug. "Why not?"

"Are you okay, Guido?" Tananda asks, peering at me sudden like. "You and Nunzio have been awfully quiet since we started out on this venture."

"We're all right," Nunzio puts in quick. "We're just a little worried about the Boss... like Massha. Joinin' the army is fine by us, if you think it will help things. Right, Guido?"

"I said it was okay, didn't I?" I snaps back at him.

"So what are you and Chumley going to be doin' while we're playing soldier?" Nunzio sez. It is obvious to me that he is out to divert the attention of the meetin' away from the two of us, but no one else seems to notice...except maybe Big Julie who gives me the hairy eyeball for a minute before turnin' his attention back to the conversation.

"We're going to see what we can do about stirring up the citizens," Tananda shrugs. "Tax reductions are nice, but there are bound to be some irritating things about life under Hemlock's new programs. All we have to do is root them out and be sure that folks see them as irritating."

"Do you blokes want Gleep, or shall we take him?" Chumley asks.

"Gleep?" sez the dragon, raisin' his head again.

"Aahh... why don't you and Tananda take him," Nunzio sez quick-like. "Truth to tell, he made me a little nervous the last time we was workin' together."

"Who? Gleep?" Tananda sez, reaching over to pet the dragon. There's nothing to be nervous about with him. He's just a big sweetie and a snugglebug...aren't you fellow?"

"Gleep!" the dragon sez again innocently while leanin' against Tananda.

"Good. Then you won't mind havin' him with you," Nunzio smiles. "That's settled."

"I suppose," Chumley sez absently, studyin' the dragon as he talks. "Well, I guess we might as well get started. Big Julie, do you mind if we relay messages to each other through you? Otherwise we're going to have trouble keeping track of things."

"No problem," the retired general shrugged. "To tell you the truth, I figure you're all going to have enough on your hands, so you shouldn't be worrying about communications. I'll be here."

After sayin' our good-byes to the others, Nunzio and I head off to try to find a recruiter for the army.

For a long time, neither of us sez anything. Finally, Nunzio clears his throat.

"Well, what do you think?"

"I think we got big trouble comin' our way," I sez, tight-lipped, "and I *don't* mean with communications or even with Queen Hemlock."

"I know what you mean," Nunzio sighs, not lookin' around as he trudges along. "You want to talk about it?"

"Not just yet. I want a little more time to think things through. In the meantime..." I aims a playful punch at him which, bein' Nunzio, he takes without so much as blinkin'. "...let's occupy ourselves with somethin' easy... like disruptin' an army."

24

Chapter 2

*"We want to make you
feel at home!"*
L. Borgia

***A**h'd like to welcome you all
to this man's army! The first thing you should
know is that we're on a first name basis here...
and my first name is **ser-geant**... Do I make
myself clear?"*

At dis, the individual so addressin' our
group pauses and glares at us. Naturally,
there's no answer, as no one is particularly eager to call attention to themselves under dese
circumstantials. It seems, however, dis was not
the response the sergeant had in mind.

*"Ah asked you a question!! Do you think
Ah'm up here running my mouth 'cause Ah like
the sound of mah own voice?"*

It is clear that dis is a ploy to induce us
new recruits into makin' a mistake which will

further anger the sergeant, as at this point he has asked not one, but two questions callin' for opposite answers, and whatever answer is given is bound to be wrong. The other unfortunates in line with Nunzio and me seem to be unaware of this and blunder headlong into the trap.

"YES, SERGEANT!" they bleat eagerly.

"WHAT??!! Are y'all tryin' to be funny?"

The sergeant, who I am glad I never had to compete against for a part in my old drama troupe, gives every impression of bein' on the verge of foamin' at the mouth and becomin' violent to the point of injurin' himself and anyone else in the near vicinity. Almost unnoticed, he has also asked a third question, placin' the odds of comin' up with an acceptable response well out of reach of the intellects in line with us.

"No... Ahh"... "Yes, Sergeant"... "Ahh... No?"

The attempt to shout an answer dissolves in a babble of confusion as the new recruits glance at each other, tryin' to sort out what they're supposed to be sayin'.

"YOU!"

The sergeant's voice silences the group's efforts as he homes in on one unfortunate in the front row.

"What are you lookin at him for? Do you think he's cute??"

"No!"

"What?"

"Ahh... No, Sergeant?"

"Ah can't hear you!"

"No, Sergeant!"

"Louder! Sound off like you got a pair!"

"NO, SERGEANT!!"

"That's better!"

The sergeant nods curtly, then turns his attention to the rest of the formation again.

Viewed correctly, dis is a fascinatin' study in group-type dynamics. By focusin' on one individual, not only has the sergeant let the rest of the group off the hook of tryin' to come up with an acceptable response to his questions, he has impressed on them that they really don't want to ever be singled out by him.

*"My name is Sergeant Smiley, and Ah will be your drill instructor for the next few days. Now, right away Ah want you to know that there are three ways of doing things in this man's army: the Right Way, the Army way, and My Way... we will do things **My way! Do I make myself clear?"***

"YES, SERGEANT!!"

The group is gettin' into the swing of things now, bellowin' out their responses like a convention of beat cops goin' after a jaywalker.

"All right now, listen up! When I call out your name, sound off loud and clear so's I know you're here and not off wandering around somewhere. Understand?"

"YES, SERGEANT!"

"Bee!"

"Here!"

"HERE WHAT?"

The kid what has just answered is so skinny it is surprisin' he can stand without assistance, but he licks his lips nervously and takes a deep breath.

"HERE, *SERGEANT!"* he shouts, but his voice cracks in the middle of it, makin' his declaration less than impressive.

"That's better," the sergeant nods, apparently satisfied with the youngster's effort. "Flie, Hyram!"

"Here, Sergeant!"

"Flie, Shubert!"

"Here, Sergeant!"

The sergeant looks up from his roster with a scowl.

"Bee? Flie? What is this, a freaking Bug Convention?"

"We're brothers, Sarge," one of the two Flies supplies unnecessarily, as the physical similarities between the two broad-shouldered individuals would be obvious even if their names didn't link them.

"That's right," the other put in. "You can call me Hy for short, and Shubert there would rather be called Shu, 'cause otherwise..."

"DID I ASK?"

"No, sir."

"Sorry, sir."

"... AND DON'T CALL ME *SIR!!!* I ain't no freakin' *officer* ! It didn't take a grant from the crown to make me a gentleman... I was *born* one!! *DO YOU UNDERSTAND ME???"*

"YES, SERGEANT!!"

"Drop down and give me twenty pushups just so you won't forget!"

"Umm... is that ten from each of us, Sarge, or..."

"TWENTY EACH!" Smiley roared. *"...AND ANOTHER FIVE EACH FOR CALLIN' ME 'SARGE!MY NAME IS SERGEANT SMILEY OR SERGEANT, NOT SARGE OR SIR! YOU GOT THAT, TROOPER??"*

"YES, SERGEANT!!"

"THEN HIT IT!!"

The two brothers drop down and start

pumpin' out pushups as the sergeant turns his attention back to his list.

"Shu Flie and Hy Flie! My aching back! My God! here's *another* one! **Spyder!**"

"Here... *Sarge.*"

Smiley's head comes up with a snap like he has been poked in the ribs... which, of course he has. The use of the improper address so soon after it was forbidden *might* have either been by mistake or from stupidity were it not for the deliberateness with which it was uttered. As it was, however, there was no mistaking it for what it was: A challenge to the sergeant's authority... which is to say, stupidity.

The challenger is a sight to behold. She probably would have stood out in the line in any case, bein' the only female-type in our group, though one might have had to look a couple times to notice, as she stood in a habitual slouch. Her hair, however, made her a real showstopper. Cropped to a medium, mane-type length, it was dyed... somethin' I do not normally speculate on regardin' a skirt until we is on very close acquaintances, after which time I am too much of a gentleman to share such information with anyone who is not. In this circumstantial, however, I feel free to make said assumption, as hair, whether attached to a male or female-type bod, does not naturally come in that color... or, to be entirely accurate, colors. Stripes of pink, white, blue, and green run across this broad's head from front to back... and not in subtle tones. These colors glow with electric-type vibrancy like they are bein' fueled by her glower, which would be truly intimidatin' if it were, perhaps, pasted on a homelier mug... like, say my own. It has been

29

some time since Nunzio and I hung out on the streets, but it is clear the type of punks they are currently breedin' is a strain mutated noticeably from our early days when 'colorful' referred to our language, *not* our hair!

"Well, well," the sergeant sez, lickin' his chops a bit," what have we here? It seems we are to be a part of the army's experimental program which is specifically testing the truth in the saying that the only thing meaner than a fighting man of Possiltum is a woman! Now I want all you *men* to watch your language during training. We have a *laaaa-dyyyy* in our midst."

From the way the skirt bristles, it is clear she is not used to bein' referred to as a lady... and doesn't care much for the idea. Smiley isn't through with her, however.

"Tell me, little lady, what *is* that you've got on your head? If it's something that crawled up there and died, I hope you've had your shots 'cause it doesn't look like it was any too healthy!"

"It's called 'hair,' *Sarge!* What do you have on *your* head?"

"It isn't what I've got on my *head* that's important, 'cruit," the sergeant smiles, "it's what's on my sleeve!"

He taps the stripes that mark his rank.

"Three up, three down. You know what that means?"

"That you're a Master Sergeant, *Sarge.*"

"Close, but no cigar. It means you owe me *fifteen pushups, 'cruit. Five for each time you've called me 'Sarge.' Hit it!"*

I expect the skirt to give him an argument at this, but instead she just drops down and starts pumpin' out pushups like it's what she has been after all along... and maybe it was. I don't know what kind of breakfast-type cereal this broad patronizes, but she is doin' a notably better job of rackin' up her pushups than the Flie brothers.

"One... Two... Three..."

Smiley watches her for a few moments, then turns his attention to the other figures on the ground.

"YOU TWO! I said give me twenty-five!"

This last was, of course, directed to the Flie brothers.

"We're... trying... sergeant!"

"WELL I CAN'T HEAR YOU! *COUNT 'EM OFF!!*"

"Seventeen... eighteen..."

"YOU DON'T START COUNTING AT SEVENTEEN!! YOU START COUNTING AT ONE!!! DO YOU THINK I'M DUMB?!!"

"No... sergeant!... One... two..."

"Now *listen up* 'cause I'm only gonna say this once!" the sergeant barks, turnin' his attention back to the rest of us. "When I'm talking, your ears are open and your mouths are **shut!** You don't say nothin' 'less I ask you a question, whereupon you answer it **briefly** then *shut up!* When I want questions from you, I'll say 'Any questions?'! *Do I make myself clear!*"

"YES, SERGEANT!"

"All right then." He started to look at his roster again, then glanced at the struggling figures on the ground. "That's enough, you three. Get back in line. Now then, where was I? Guido!"

"Here, Sergeant!" I sez, 'cause I was.

"That's it? Just 'Guido?' No nickname like Cricket or anything?"

"No, Sergeant!"

He waited for a few seconds to see if I was gonna add anything, but I didn't, as I've always been a fast study. Finally he gives a little nod and moves on.

"Juney!"

"Here, Sergeant! ...but folks call me 'Junebug.' "

Some people, on the other hand, never seem to learn.

"Twenty!" the sergeant sez without even lookin' up from the roster.

And so it went. By the time the sergeant is through checkin' off the list of names, over half of our group has been called upon to demonstrate their physical prowess, or lack thereof, by performin' a number of pushups, the exact count of which varies dependin' upon the sergeant's mood and their ability to remember to count out loud whilst performin' this exercise. This raises some serious questions in my mind as to the average IQ of the individuals who have chosen to enlist in the army, a rather disquietin' thought realizin' that I am one of said individuals. In an effort to maintain a positive-type frame of mind, I reassure myself that my enlistin' was a matter of followin' orders rather than any idea of my own.

"All right, *LISTEN UP!*" the sergeant bellows, havin' finished with his roll call. "In about half an hour, Corporal Whittle will take you across camp and get your hair cut to conform with army standards."

The little shrimp who has been lurkin' in the background draws himself up to his full insignificant height and smiles at this. Now Sergeant Smiley is a rather imposin' dude, though a touch out of shape around the middle, but the corporal looks like he would fail the entrance requirements to be a meter-type maid. That is, he looks to be the unpleasant kind of wimp who only pulls wings off flies when he has enough rank to back him up. Lookin' at his smile, I begin to have serious misgivin's about these haircuts.

"In the meantime," the sergeant continues, "you have a period of unstructured time, during which you may talk, sleep, or get to know each other. I suggest you take maximum advantage of this, as it will in all probability be the last time you will have to yourself until your training is completed. Now, before I dismiss you, are there any questions?"

To my surprise, two individuals raise their hands. This is a surprise first of all because I thought that most individuals would be cowed into silence by the sergeant's performance thus far, and secondly because one of the hands belongs to none other than my cousin Nunzio!

"You!" Smiley says, pointin' at the closest questioner. "State your name and question."

"Bee, Sergeant. I... I think there's been a mistake on my enlistment."

The sergeant shows all his teeth.

"The army doesn't make mistakes, son... except, maybe one." He shoots a glance at Spyder, who ignores him this time. "What's your problem?"

"Well... I shouldn't be here. I enlisted as a magician, and my recruiter said that..."

The sergeant's smile widens sufficiently to stop the recruit in mid-sentence.

"Son," he sez, in a voice that's more like a purr, "it's time you learned one of the harsh truths about the army. *Recruiters lie!* Whatever that sorry soul told you, son, unless you got it in writing signed by the queen herself, it don't mean squat! Now *I'm* telling you that every 'cruit that signs onto this man's army *will* learn basic infantry skills before receivin' his first assignment before active duty. You *might* get assigned as a magician, or you might not... it all depends on whether they need magicians or cooks when your number comes up for assignment, but you aren't gonna get assigned *anywhere* until *I* say your basic training is complete. *Next question!*"

"Nunzio, Sergeant! How long does it take to complete basic training?"

"That depends on how long it takes you unfortunates to learn the minimal skills required for you to wear the uniform of Possiltum. Usually it takes a week to ten days... but from the looks of you sorry souls, I figure you'll have the pleasure of my company for at least a month."

"You mean none of us gets assigned until everyone in this group completes their training?"

"That's right. Any other questions?"

My cousin glances down the line at me, but I keep my eyes straight forward, hopin' his action isn't noticed. Luckily the sergeant misses this little blip in the formation, and as soon as he dismisses us Nunzio and I go into a huddle.

"What do you think?" he sez, worried-like.

"Same as you," I shrug. "We sure can't take no month gettin' trained if we're gonna be any help upsettin' the regular troops."

34

"That's for sure," he nods. "Looks like we're gonna have to push these recruits a little ourselves to be sure they pick up this training in double-quick time."

This realization puts my mood at an all-time low. It was bad enough that I was gonna have to do time as a soldier-type, but now I was gonna have to play nursemaid and coach to a bunch of raw recruits as well!

Chapter 3

"Just a little off the top!"
A. Boleyn

The haircut turned out even more ghastly than I had feared in my worst nightmare-type dreams. I would be tempted to lay in wait and inflict a little instructional-type revenge upon the individual what laid said haircut on me, but it would probably do no good as he was obviously brain damaged at birth and can't help bein' like he is. Instead, I should be thankful that society has found a place for a person what has only learned one style of haircut where he can serve a useful purpose. Further, I suppose it is only logical that that place is in the army, where his "customers" have no choice but to put up with whatever haircut they are given. My only puzzlement is where they managed to find an en-

tire room full of mental deficients who have all
only learned the same haircut.

The haircut under discussion is unique in
its lack of imagination and style, consistin' of
simply removin' as much hair from the victim
as possible through the vigorous application of
a pair of clippers. If they lowered their aim another quarter inch or so, the job would qualify
as a scalpin' rather than as a haircut. Now, I
have nothin' against baldness, and know a
couple hard-type wiseguys in the mob what
shave their heads to look especially mean.
What we ended up with, however, was not
enough hair to look stylish, but too much to
look tough.

Now this in itself was annoyin', but the

37

haircut in conjunction with the uniforms which was foisted off on us bordered on bein' intolerable. For those of youse which are fortunate enough not to have viewed the Possiltum army uniforms first hand, they consist of somethin' like a short-sleeved flannel nightshirt, which is worn under a combination breastplate and skirt made of hardened leather. That's right, a skirt. At least, I can't think of any other way to describe a bunch of leather strips hangin' down to about knee length with no semblance of legs built in. As a final insult, we was each issued a pair of sandals, which to my opinion did not even come close to replacin' the spiffy wing-tipped black and white shoes I normally favor.

The overall impression of our trainin' group once we had been shorn and uniformed, was that we looked like a pack of half-dressed department store mannequins waitin' to be fitted for wigs.

"Nunzio," I sez, surveyin' the damage what has been done to my hitherto head-turnin' image, "tell me again about how nothin' is too desperate when it comes to guardin' the Boss or carryin' out his orders."

Now, this is a mistake. While my cousin is a first-rate partner when it comes to rough and tumble, lurkin' in the depths of his sordid resumé is the fact that he did time as a school-teacher for a while, and the lingerin' effect of that experience is that he has a tendency to deliver lectures on nearly any subject at the drop of a hat or a straight-type line.

"You just don't understand the psychology involved in converting civilians to soldiers, Guido," he sez in that squeaky voice of his that can be so irritatin' at times... like now. "Hair styles, like fashions in clothing, are distinctive marks of one's previous social and financial standing. The whole idea of the haircuts and uniforms is to reduce everyone to a common denominator, as well as giving them a traumatic, but harmless, experience to share, thereby encouraging bonding."

Normally, I would not dream of arguin' with Nunzio, as I not only am inclined to lose, it only gives him an excuse to prolong and embellish upon whatever half-baked theory he is emotin' upon. This time, however, I feels compelled to take umbrage with his assertions.

"Cousin," I sez, "can you look around at our fellow unfortunates and tell me honestly that you can't tell who comes from where without committin' such blatant perjury that even the most bought judge would have to call youse on it?"

I mean, shorn and frocked as we are, it is still pretty easy to spot who the players are and where they're comin' from. The Flie brothers have that well muscled, robust glow of health what only comes from puttin' so many hours a day into farm work that doin' time in the army has to look like a resort vacation to them. Bee, with or without hair, looks like a fledgling geek, and as for the Spyder broad... well, givin' a wolf a poodle cut doesn't make it look like a show dog, just like a pissed off wolf! It was clear to me that wherever that junior sociopath went to school, it couldn't have been more than a block or two from the alma mother what gave Nunzio and me our head start on the other head bashers in the Mob.

As usually occurs, however, just when it looks like I'm gonna finally win an argument with Nunzio, somethin' intervenes to change the subject.

"Do you believe this?" the tough broad spits... literally... lettin' fly with an impressive jet of fluid from between her teeth to punctuate her anger. "Military Law! It's bad enough that we have to put up with these haircuts and flaky uniforms, but now we have to sit through lectures on crud like Military Law! When are they gonna get around to teaching us something about fighting?"

This does not come as a particularly startlin' revelation to me, as I have long suspected that Spyder did not enlist for the cultural-type benefits that the army offers. I am, however, more than a little taken with the distance she gets with her spittin'. It occurs to me that I haven't tried spittin' that way since Don Bruce promoted us and hinted strongly that we should class up our act a little, and, realizin' this, decide not to try to match her performance, as distance spittin' such as hers requires constant practice if one is to remain in form. For the educatin' of those of youse what has been raised too proper and upright to have ever experimented with this particular form of self-expression, let me caution youse against tryin' this for the first time in front of a critical audience. If your technique is anythin' less than flawless, the odds are that your effort will dribble down your chin and onto your shirt rather than arcin' away in the picturesque display you was expectin', leavin' the viewers with an impression of youse as a chump rather than whatever it was youse was tryin' to pass yourself off as.

All of this passes through my mind in a

flash, as I am a fairly quick thinker despite the impression given by my size, whilst I am tryin' to think of an appropriate response to Spyder's kvetchin'. Nunzio comes up with somethin' before I do, however, as he is no slouch himself when it comes to thinkin'... particularly when there is a skirt involved.

"I think you should listen *real* close to what they tell us about Military Law, Spyder," he sez, "it'll pay some solid benefits in the long run."

"How so?"

"Well," he smiles, settlin' into his lecture voice again, "speaking from long personal experience, it is often much easier to continue doing exactly what you want to do right under the noses of authority if one is aware of exactly what those authorities consider to be antisocial behavior. When you stop to think about it, it's real nice of the army to give us official advance warning of exactly what rules they plan to enforce and, by exclusion, what is fair game. If they didn't, or we were dumb enough to sleep through this particular lecture, the only way to figure out what activities can be done openly and which should be performed in... shall we say, a less public manner, would be to act blindly, then wait to see what they came down on us for."

"Just how long *is* that 'personal experience,' fellah?" one of the Flie brothers pipes up.

"Yeah, I was just wondering the same thing," the other chimes in. "Aren't you two a little *old* to be joining the army?"

Now, it is clear to me what is goin' on. The two farm boys have been hopin' to put some moves on Spyder, but then Nunzio gets in the way. Rather than backin' off like any sane person would do, they was tryin' to score their points by pickin' a fight with him. To say the least, I have seen better plans to continue one's good health.

Of course, Nunzio can spot it too, and he knows that we should be avoidin' any kind of trouble if we want to complete our training quick instead of sittin' in the stockade for a few days. He also knows, however, that he is bein' made to look like a fool in front of the only skirt we is likely to be associatin' with for a while, and while he has considerable tolerance at soakin' up abuse from a boss what is payin' our wages and expenses, his ability to put up with bein' hassled without blowin' his cool drops in direct proportion to the standin' of the hassler in the peckin' order, and the Flie brothers don't stand very high at all.

"Are you boys sayin' you think we're too old to be any good in a fight?" he sez, turnin' to face his critics while flexin' his hands slightly.

If I didn't recognize the dangerous tone in his voice, I could sure recognize that flexin' action of his as as I was the one who taught it to him in the first place, and figure I had better step in before things get too messy.

"Before proceedin' with the discussion at hand," I sez, "I think youse should all perhaps take notice of the attention which is bein' paid to our intellectual-type conversation by the corporal who is standin' not twenty yards behind youse."

" 'Intellectual-type discussion'?" Shu brays, punchin' his brother on the arm. "What kind of talk is that, Old Man?"

"Paw told us big city folk talked kinda funny," Hy grinned, "but I ain't never heard *nobody* who sounds as weird as this guy."

"He's talked that way ever since he played one of the leads in "Guys and Dolls" while we was in college," Nunzio sez, quick-like. "Beyond that, I strongly suggest you drop the subject."

That's when I realize that I have commenced to flex my own hands a bit... an action which has the tendency to make Nunzio nervous. While I am not particularly sensitive to callous or ignorant remarks about my size or how I'm gettin' older, I *can* get a little touchy if anyone tries to poke fun at how I talk. You see, I have spent considerable time perfectin' this particular style of expression as I feel it enhances my believability as a rough and tumble leg-breaker, thereby minimizing the number of times I have to actually partake of the violent-type actions which so offend and depress my sensitive soul. Therefore, anyone who tries to state or imply that talkin' like dis is easy or stupid is issuin' an invitation to waltz with me which would best be withheld unless his or her hospitalization insurance is substantial, detailed, and paid up. This is, of course, the very button the Flie brothers is tinkerin' with, and I find their efforts sufficiently clumsy as to require immediate instruction as to the error of their ways and perhaps a little behavioral adjustment. The fact that I am still annoyed over the haircuts and uniforms and sorta lookin' for someone to take it out on has completely nothin' to do with my reactions.

"Were you in that musical, too?" Junebug sez, unwittingly steppin' between us in his eagerness to start a conversation. He is a good-lookin' kid with the kind of soft, unblemished features usually associated with male fashion-type models. "I got to play Sky Masterson, my-self. What was your major, anyway? I got my Bachelor's in Dance."

"BusAd... a Master's," I sez, tryin to ease around him.

Unfortunately he has given the Flie broth-ers a face-savin' out from the buildin' confron-tation with Nunzio and me. Whether motivated by any native intelligence or simply saved by animal survival instinct, they switch their har-assment to this new target without so much as pausin' for breath."

"A college man? ...And a dancer! Ooooo! Did you hear that, Hy?"

"Sure did," his brother responds and com-mences to make kissey noises at Junebug. "No wonder he's so purdy."

"Leave him alone, you guys!"

This last comes from Spyder, who for some reason has seen fit to deal herself into the situational.

"Oh yeah?" Shu sneers, turnin' his atten-tion toward this new front. "And who's going to make me?"

"If I have to, I will," Spyder shoots back.

"Oh yeah?"

"Yeah!"

"Well then, why don't you show us... OW!"

By now I have cooled off enough to take advantage of the situational as it presents it-self. As they puff up and start to strut toward Spyder, the two brothers have thoughtlessly and rudely turned their backs on me. Before they can close on her, I have stepped in behind and between them, and dropped a friendly arm around their shoulders.

"Excuse me, Spyder," I sez with a smile,

"but I need to have a few words with these boys in private whilst they are still able to stand and walk without the aid of crutch-type assistance. Right boys?"

"OW!... Right!"

"Yeah... Aaah!... Sure!"

The sudden cooperative nature of the Flie brothers is in no small way influenced by the fact that I have casually dug a thumb into the hollow of a collarbone on each of them and tend to tighten my grip another notch each time I asks them a question... regardless of how rhetorical it might be. The real trick to this maneuver, in case any of youse is interested in technical-type details, is not to loosen your grip once you start tightenin' it. That is, it isn't squeeze... release... squeeze... release..., it's squeeze... tighten... tighter... *grind*.... See what I mean? Now if, perhaps, youse have developed your grip to a point where you can crumble bricks with it... like I have... this will prove to be a most convincin' punctuation to the weakest of logic durin' a difference of opinion.

Anyhoo, returnin' to my oration, I draws the two brothers aside for a little chat, all the while keepin' a wary eye on the hoverin' corporal.

"Now, don't you think it would be a good idea for you boys to lighten up a little? (squeeze)" I sez softly so's we are the only ones who can hear. "There are two things you should be considerin' here. First, dis collection of individuals we is goin' through trainin' with constitutes a group, and within a group it is always better to be nice than nasty. With nice, you got friends who will cover your back in a fight... with nasty, youse gotta watch your back from them. You got that? (tighten)"

"Right, Guido!"

"OW! Sure Guido!"

"Good. Now second, I want youse to keep in mind that if you does *not* abandon your querulous habits, and those habits slow or otherwise interfere with this group completin' its trainin' in the shortest possible time..." I sneak a glance at the corporal, then lower my voice while takin' great pains to keep a smile on my face. "...then I will *personally* rip off each of youse guy's heads and spit down your neck! (tighter) You got that?"

"Gaah! Yeah! Got it!"

"Anything you... Owwww... say, Guido!"

"Oh yeah. Just one more thing. *I don't talk funny* (grind) Agreed?"

"Aaaahhhh..."

"God..."

I notice the corporal is comin, our way, thereby signalin' an end to our playtime.

"I'll take that as a 'yes,' " I sez, and releases my grip all at once.

I have neglected to mention durin' my previous instructional oration that if youse relaxes the aforementioned grip suddenly and completely, the resultin' rush of blood to the area which has been assaulted by said grip causes additional discomfort to a point where some subjects have been known to faint dead away. The advantage of this is obvious, in that you are not actually even touching them at the moment the effect takes hold.

The Flie brothers are in exceptionally good shape, as I have noted before, so they merely stagger a bit. It is clear to them, however, as it is to me, that for a while they will have extreme difficulty movin' their arms with any degree of speed or strength... like say, in a fight. This, of course, has the originally desired effect of mellowin' their previously bullyin', swaggerin' behavior noticeably.

"What's going on here?" the corporal demands, burstin' in on our little group.

I blinks innocent-like and give him a helpless shrug like he was a DA during cross examination.

"We was just discussin' the logical-type benefits of social over antisocial behavior in a group situational."

"Oh yeah? Is that right, you two?"

The Flies try to match my shrug, but wince halfway through the gesture and have to resort to nods.

The corporal glares at us suspiciously for a few, then turns to the rest of the group.

"All right, everybody form up in two lines!" he hollers in a poor imitation of the sergeant. "It's time we move out for the classrooms!"

"Did our agitators respond properly to applied logic?" Nunzio murmurs, easin' up beside me.

"Sure did," I nods. "What's more, I think they got it in one lesson. I don't know why you keep sayin' that youth today is slow learners."

He rolls his eyes at this and fakes a mock swing at me.

"Maybe we should start calling you 'Fly Swatter,' " he grins.

Some of the other recruits laugh at this, which makes me a tad nervous, as I know from the Mob just how easy it is to get saddled with a screwball nickname after some dumb incident or other. The corporal saved me the trouble of havin' to change the subject, however, as he chose that moment to start hollerin' and wavin' for us to get together for the next round of trainin'.

"Come on," I sez, bouncin' a punch off his arm that was notably harder than the one he had taken at me. "We gotta go learn how to be effective fighters."

Chapter 4

"Squeeze, don't jerk, the trigger."
R. Rogers

Unfortunately, the "Fly Swatter" moniker Nunzio hung on me stuck... or at least the "Swatter" part did. What was even more discomfortin' was the fact that I got tagged by the sergeant to be Actin' Squad Leader for the little group of recruits I have already named, which is much of why I named them. This position consisted of nothin' more than playin' sheepdog for the 'Bugs,' as everyone seemed to take great delight in callin' 'em, while they was bein' herded from one trainin' session to another. Still, it was a leadership position, which, as I have earlier noted, I tend to avoid like I would a subpoena.

The stuff we had to learn as part of our basic-type trainin' wasn't really too bad, though. Most of the information they passed along was indeed necessary when considered as an overview, and it was presented simply, but with a real effort toward makin' it interestin' enough to hold the attention of us recruits. This was a pleasant change from my college profs, most of whom seemed to feel they was the greatest experts on the most interestin' subjects and that the students should feel lucky to pay substantial hunks of money for the privilege of worshipin' at their feet. What's more, they tested the loyalty of said students on a regular basis by the simple process of makin' the presentation dull enough to bore a stone and seein' who managed to stay awake long enough to absorb sufficient data to pass their finals.

The army, in direct contrast, started with the basic assumption that recruits would be totally ignorant and couldn't care less about the subject at hand, unless it was made interestin' enough to hold their predictably short attention, often by graphically demonstratin' at a personal level how vital said subject was to the continued functioning of their bodies.

(Out of courtesy to those of youse who are currently investin' large hunks of your or your kid's time in college, I will refrain on commentin' on which system I think is better for passin' information, much less the actual life value of that information which is bein' passed, and confine myself to the simple observation that instruction in the army is neither mindless nor lackin' in value. What's more, *they* pay *you* while you're learnin'. Of course, things might be quite a bit different if corporations other than fast food franchisers took it upon themselves to take an active hand in the trainin' of their employees... but that is a whole 'nother subject and a definite digression from the subject at hand, which is army trainin'.)

For the most part, Nunzio and I had no complaints with the lessons, and even found them uniquely informational. As youse are probably aware, the Mob is big on individual tactics or free-for-all-type brawls such as is usually the case in ambushes, so learnin' to fight from formations was a genuinely new experience for us. Of course, we had some difficulty acceptin' that this would ever be of actual use to us.

Firstus, as I have just so previously mentioned, bodyguardin' usually involves ambushes and what is known in sports as "scramble defense," raisin' serious doubts in our mind that formation fightin would be utilizable in our civilian life after the service, seein' as how we would lack the warm-type bodies for such maneuvers, and it is doubtful those throwin' the surprise party would give us sufficient time to gather the necessary quantities of warm bodies, as the entire purpose of their ambush is to catch us with our tactical pants around our ankles.

Secondous, and more to the point, however, it was unclear how we was supposed to use these tactics while in the army. You see, at this point it was no secret that the army of Possiltum was the largest, best equipped force around, so few kingdoms or towns chose to buck the long odds by confrontin' them in the field where formation-type tactics would come into play. Consequentially, there was little actual fightin' goin' on when they moved into a new neighborhood, an any opposition offered was more on the order of covertous resistance of the stab-em-in-the-back or slit-their-throats-while-they're-asleep-type variety. As formations were of absolutely no use in dealin' with this kind of petty harassment, it was hard for us to understand why we was havin' to spend so much time learnin' about them.

Somehow, however, Sergeant Smiley neglects to ask our advice as to the content of his trainin' program, so we are spared the discomfort of havin' to figure out how to share our views with him without hurtin' his feelin's.

Similarly, when it is explained to us that we has to learn marchin' as it is "the best way to move a group of soldiers from one point to another in the shortest period of time," we are not given a chance to ask if the army in general or the sergeant in specific has considered the benefits of rapid transit.

While there are numerous points like this of dubious logic throughout our trainin' there is only one point which we take serious exception to. While we take great pains to keep this variation from army thinkin' from becomin' obvious, it finally escapes into the light of public notice one day while we are at the firin' range.

The army is havin' us train with crossbows... which is understandable, as the trainin' time necessary for usin' a longbow with any degree of proficiency in a combat situational is considerable, thereby makin' it a dubious subject of study for basic trainin'. Slings is even worse, as until one has reached near expert familiarity with one, the best odds of inflictin' injury with this weapon is that of hangin' oneself with said weapon whilst tryin' to get the rock to fly somewhere near the general direction of the target. The most physically inept of klutzes, however can attain a minimal level of effectiveness with a crossbow in a single afternoon, which is doubtlessly why the army chose this particular weapon to introduce the recruits to the intricacies of projectile combat.

"You will notice that you will be firing at full sized, man-shaped targets for this exercise," Sergeant Smiley says, havin' already bellowed at length on range safety and proper handlin' of the weapons. "The army has chosen to have you train on these as opposed to bull's-eyes, as it will better prepare you mentally and emotionally to fire your weapon at a live opponent. At all times during this exercise, you will fix it in your minds that the dummy facing you is a live enemy who wants to kill you, and conduct yourselves accordingly. Do I make myself clear?"

"YES, SERGEANT!!"

The crew has this response down pat now... and it only took 'em a few days of trainin' to master it. Nunzio and me joins in at the proper cue, though there are some questions which could have been raised at this point.

For example, while the idea behind usin' these targets was interestin' and maybe even admirable, in all my years with the Mob I have never seen an opponent who would do you the favor of standin' rock-still, in the open, upright, with his shoulders square to you while he was tryin' to shoot you. They are more inclined to be crouched or flattened behind cover and movin' around whilst sendin' you the message, specifically to minimize the chances of your

53

cancelin' their stamp before they reach the final salutation. In light of this, thinkin' you can shoot because you can pump arrows or quarrels into a straw dummy of any shape struck me as a dangerous case of overconfidence and not to be encouraged. I kept quiet about this, though, figurin' that this was only the first round to familiarize everybody with their weapons, and that the *serious* trainin' would be covered at a later date.

Soon, the crew is scattered along the firin' line, takin' turns sprayin' quarrels downrange whilst the sergeant and corporal prowl back and forth behind them, qualifyin' some and hollerin' at the slow learners. This is one managerial style I have noticed the army and the Mob have in common, which is to say the belief that if you shout loud enough at someone who is doin' somethin' wrong, they will respond by doin' it right.

Nunzio and me hang back from the first bunch of shooters, as we have little fear of passin' this particular test. We focus instead on how the rest of the crew is doin' so's we can help out the ones what is havin' trouble.

The Flie brothers are surprisingly good shots, each of them not only hittin' the target with every shot, but holdin' a shot group you can cover with a double handspan. Realizin' that the targets are close enough to hit with a rock, however, this display of marksmanship fails to impress me a great deal. Sergeant Smiley, on the other hand, seems genuinely pleased with their performance.

"Now *that's* how the army likes to see you handle those weapons! he sez loud so's everyone can hear him. "Who taught you boys to

54

shoot like that, anyway?"

"Our dad did," Shu Flie grins. "You may have heard of him. They call him Horse Flie."

"Mom can outshoot him, though," Hy Flie adds. "They call her Dragon Flie."

At this point, I stopped followin' the conversation, both because it was makin' my stomach hurt, and because Nunzio was beckonin' me to huddle up with him.

"We got problems," he sez, which wasn't surprisin', as knowin' him as well as I do I could see he was worried.

"Like what?"

"It's Spellin' Bee," he sez, which is what we've taken to callin' our junior magician. "I don't think he could hit the broadside of a barn if he was inside it."

I snuck a look over his shoulder, just in time to see Bee loose a quarrel which misses the target by fifteen feet, give or take a mile. The corporal was right there beside him, offering helpful suggestions at the top of his lungs.

"I see. Well, it's not like he's gonna do much shootin', what with him bein' a magician."

"Maybe not," Nunzio shrugs, "but we're all supposed to qualify today or the whole group gets held back... remember?

"That could be a problem," I nods. "Doesn't he have a spell or somethin' that could help him out?"

My cousin rolls his eyes and snorts, disgusted-like.

"Are you kidding? He only knows two spells, and neither of them are gonna be of any help to him on the firing line."

"Two spells? What are they?"

"Let's see, he knows Dispell, which lets him see through disguise spells."

"That's not much help," I admits. "What's his other spell?"

"Datspell," Nunzio grimaces, "which is nothing more than the disguise spell the Boss uses with a silly name."

"So all he can do is disguise himself and see through other disguises." I sez, turnin' it over in my mind.

"That's it. Nothin' that's gonna help him qualify today."

"Maybe... maybe not," I sez, thoughtfully. "Tell you what. Is there any chance you can get him alone for a a few minutes?"

"No problem. When he finishes blowin' this round, he'll have to wait to take another turn. I can get him then. Why? You got an idea?

"Uh-huh," I grins. "Just convince him to use his disguise spell... what does he call it? Oh yeah, Datspell... so's you can change places. Then *you* qualify for him, you switch back, and no one will be any the wiser."

"I dunno," Nunzio sez, rubbin' his chin. "We might be able to fool the corporal, but the sergeant there's a pretty sharp cookie. He might spot there's somethin' different about the Bee."

"I'll take care of distractin' the sergeant when the time comes. Just be careful not to shoot *too* good... just good enough to qualify. Got it?"

Then there isn't much to do whilst waiting for the plan to unfold. Finally the corporal gets fed up with shoutin' at our young magician and sends him off the line for a "break" until he has rested his voice a bit.

Tryin' not to pay too much attention, I watch out of the corner of my eye while Nunzio drapes an arm around Bee's shoulder and begins to talk to him in an earnest-type fashion, all the while leadin' him casually behind the weapon storage tent and out of general sight. After what seems like an intolerably long time, "Bee" re-emerges, walkin' in a rollin' stride that is very familiar to me, and I know the power of reason and logic has triumphed again. I wait until he is steppin' up to the firin' line for yet another try, then commence to create a diversion.

"You're tryin' too hard, Spyder," I sez, loud-like, steppin' up behind that notable where she is standin' at the far end of the firin' line from "Bee."

Both Spyder and Junebug are sporadic in their marksmanship, keepin' their shots in the vicinity of the target, but only hittin' it occasionally.

"You're keepin' your left arm way too tense... you gotta loosen up a little and just cradle the weapon in your hand. Ease up on the trigger, too. Just use the tip of your finger instead of tryin to wrap it all the way around the trigger. Otherwise, you'll pull your shot off to the left every time you squeeze off a round."

"Like this?"

"Yeah, only.."

"WHAT THE HECK YA THINK YOU'RE DOIN??!!"

It should have been gratifying' to know that I was correct in my appraisal of Sergeant Smiley's boilin' point. Up until now, Nunzio and me have been real careful to do our coachin' of the other recruits out of his sight and hearin', so's not to conflict with the authority-type image he is workin' so hard to maintain. I figure that this open display will not sit well with him, and this figurin' proves to be dead on target. I should be glad, but as he comes stompin' toward me I have to fight off the sneakin' feelin' that this has not been the wisest tactic to pursue.

"Guido was just giving me some pointers on handling this thing, Sergeant," Spyder sez, innocent-like, her polite manners a testimony to her hard learned lessons that Smiley is not someone to hassle unnecessarily.

"Oh, so now the Bug Swatter's an expert on crossbows, is he?" the sergeant snarls, puttin' the cross hairs on me. "Thinks he's better'n me or the range instructors at teaching marksmanship, does he?"

While trackin' this with great attention, I nonetheless see over his shoulder that Nunzio, disguised as Bee, is firin' his qualifyin' round... right under the nose of the corporal, who is more interested in watchin' the sergeant and me than in payin' attention to what's happenin' at his end of the range.

"Why don't you just show us how good you are with this weapon, *acting* Squad Leader Guido," Smiley sez, snatchin' the crossbow away from Spyder and thrustin' it at me. "*If* you can qualify, then *maybe* I won't bust you back into the ranks."

Now I have been threatened by experts... literally... so this effort by the sergeant fails to generate in me the obviously desired nervousness. If anything, I am tempted to deliberately blow these shots, thereby gettin' myself off the leadership-type hook which, as I have noted

58

earlier, I am not particularly happy to be dan-
glin' from. Still, my professional abilities have
been openly challenged... and in front of a
skirt, even it it's just Spyder. Besides, Nunzio
has now finished qualifyin' for Bee, so there is
no incentive to prolong this diversion any
longer.

I spare the crossbow no more than a cur-
sory glance, havin' a weak stomach when it
comes to substandard weapons. It is obviously
the work of government contractors, and bears
the same resemblance to the custom weapons
from Iolo that I normally use that a plow horse
bears to a thoroughbred. Ignorin' this, I holds a
quarrel in my mouth while cockin' the crossbow by puttin' the butt in my stomach and
jerkin' the string back with both hands (which
is quicker'n usin' the foot stirrup to do the
same thing), drop the quarrel into the groove
ahead of the drawn string, and squeeze off a
quick shot down range.

Not surprisin'ly, the missile *thwacks* into
the dummy's right shoulder.

"A bit lucky, but not bad," Smiley sez,
grudgin' like. "You'd get better accuracy,
though, if you shot from the shoulder instead
of the hip. Trying to show off will only..."

By the time he gets this far in his critique,
I have recocked, reloaded, and loosed a second
shot... again workin' from the hip.

This shot hisses into place not more than
two finger widths from the first.

The sergeant shuts his mouth so fast you
can hear his teeth click together, which is fine
by me, and watches in silence whilst I snap a
third shot off that makes a neat triangle with
the first two.

"Pretty sloppy," comes the sneerin' squeak of Nunzio, as he joins our group, free of his disguise now. "I warned you that crushing stuff with your hands was gonna ruin your touch for a trigger!"

"Izzat so!!??" I snaps, more than a little annoyed at havin' my handiwork decried. "Let's see you do better with this thing!"

I lob the crossbow to him, which he catches with one hand, then squints at the bindings.

"Government contractors," he sez in the same tone he uses to announce he's stepped in somethin' organic and unpleasant. "It sure ain't Iolo's work!"

"The quarrels are about as straight as a barroom pool cue, too," I sez, givin' him the rest of the bad news. "But like the Boss sez: 'Ya does the best ya can with what ya got.' Right?"

He makes a face at me, then snaps off his three shots, also shootin' from the hip. I notice that even though he works the dummy's other shoulder to avoid confusion, his groupin' is not a noticeable improvement over mine.

"Okay, it's the weapon... *this* time," he admits, handin' the crossbow back to Spyder. "If we were working a longer range, though, I still think..."

"Just a minute, you two!"

We turns our attention to the sergeant, both because he sounds upset over somethin', and because we've been havin' this particular argument for years, so it's doubtful we would have resolved anythin' even if we had continued the discussion uninterrupted.

"What are you trying to pull, here?"

"What's wrong, Sergeant?" Nunzio sez, ex-

pressin' the puzzlement we both is feelin'. "Two out of three hits qualifies, right?"

"What's wrong?" Smiley smiles, showin' too many teeth for comfort. "Shot groupings like those mean you've both got excellent control of your weapons. Now, correct me if I'm mistaken, but doesn't that also mean you could have put those groupings anywhere on the target you wanted?"

"Well, sure... Sergeant."

"So how come you shot the dummy in the shoulders instead of in the head or chest?"

"That would kill him," I sez before I've had a chance to think it through.

"YOU'RE SUPPOSED TO KILL HIM! THAT'S

61

WHAT BEIN' A SOLDIER IS ALL ABOUT!!!"

Now, in hindsight I know I shoulda' gone along with him, but he caught me by surprise, and my old Mob-type habits cut in.

"What kinda cheap barroom shooters do you take us for??"" I barks right back at him. *"Me and Nunzio is professionals!! Any jerk can kill somebody, but it takes SKILL to leave 'em in a condition where they can still pay protection... OR give you information... OR... "*

"What my cousin *means* to say," Nunzio sez, steppin' between us quick-like, "is that wounding an enemy takes *three* opponents out of the action instead of just one, since someone's got to help him get back to... "

It was a good try, but too late. The sergeant was still into takin' me on.

"Are you calling the trained soldiers of Possiltum jerks?" he hollers, steppin' around Nunzio to come at me again. *"What are you? Some kind of PACIFIST?"*

"What... did... you... call... me...?" I sez in my softest voice, which I only use on special occasions.

The trainin' area around us suddenly got real quiet and still... except for Nunzio who gave a disbelievin' whistle through his teeth as he stepped back.

Somethin' in my voice or the way I was drawin' myself up to my full height must have triggered the sergeant's survival instinct, 'cause all of a sudden he looked around nervous-like as if he were tryin' to find an emergency exit door.

"WHAT ARE YOU ALL DOING JUST STANDING AROUND??!!!" he bellows, turnin' his attention from me to the crowd which has gathered

around us. *"YOU'RE SUPPOSED TO BE QUALI-FYING!! MOVE IT!!! NOW!!!"*

This interruption gives me time to get my temper under control, and, after coolin' down a bit, I decide it is just as well the episode has drawn to a close. It seems, however, that the sergeant has a few last words for me.

"Guido!" he sez, just loud enough for me to hear, not lookin' me in the face.

"Yeah, Sergeant?"

"This isn't the time or the place, but we *will* continue this discussion... later."

The way he said it, it wasn't a challenge or a threat... just a statement.

Chapter 5

*"When I travel, nobody knows me...
and I like it that way!"*
S. King

Nunzio and me was tryin' to figure out what it was they had put on our plates under the laughin' title of "dinner," when Spyder plops down next to us. We're a little surprised at this, as we're normally left to ourselves when dinin', but the reason for her forwardness in not long in comin'.

"You guys are with the Mob, aren't you," she sez, without so much as a 'Hello' or 'Nice evening.' "

Now, way back in the intro, I mentioned that we are not real big on bein' asked questions in general, and this specific question is a definite no-no.

"Are you a cop?" Nunzio shoots back, automatic-like.

This is a 'Must Learn' question for anyone whose livelihood depends on extra-legal activities, as if one asks it of a cop, however undercover they might be, they have to acknowledge their profession. Otherwise, any attempt to use the followin' conversation as evidence is dismissed as entrapment.

"Me? Are you kidding? No, I'm not a cop. Why do you ask?"

"Why do you want to know if we're in the Mob?" Nunzio shoots back.

You will notice that at this point, Spyder has answered our question, but we have not yet given a 'yea' or 'nay' to hers. Like I say, one has an inclination towards caginess in our line of work. Maybe it's a habit resultin' from our regular and prolonged discussions with DAs and Grand Juries.

"I've been thinking of trying to join up with them once I get out of the army," she sez with a shrug. "I thought maybe you guys could give me a little information about what it's like workin' for the Mob, if not give me a recommendation or at least a contact."

"Connection."

"What's that, Swatter?"

"I said 'Connection.' In normal business you have contacts. In the Mob, the first step is to get 'connected.' "

"...Or so we've heard." Nunzio sez quicklike, givin' me one of his dirty looks. "I dunno. We might be able to share a few rumors with you. What do you want to know?"

As you can see, my cousin is still bein' cautious, havin' less faith than I do in a 'hearsay' defense. With his 'rumor' gambit, however, he has opened the door for us to answer a few questions bout the Mob *without* actually admittin' to any affiliation on our part.

"Well, what's it like?"

"The hours are lousy," I sez.

"...And the retirement plan leaves a lot to be desired," Nunzio adds.

"...But the pay's good. Right?" Spyder urges.

I have mentioned before that my cousin has few loves greater than the desire to lecture, and this chick has just pushed one of his favorite buttons. While he does not relax completely, he defrosts a bit.

"Not as good as you'd think from what the media says," he squeaks. "You see... remember what Guido said a second ago about being connected? Well, for a long time, when you first join the Mob, you actually have to pay us... strike that... *them* instead of the other way around."

"How's that again?"

"It's easier to understand if you think of it as a franchise system. The Mob gives you permission or license to operate, and you give them a share of your profits. You have to give a percentage, say half, to the guy over you, who in turn has to split with the guy over him, and so on right up to the top. Of course, the guys at the top pull down a bundle, since there's a whole pyramid under them feeding 'em percentages."

"Wait a minute!" Spyder frowns. "The last time I heard something like this, they were trying to get me to sell cosmetics... or was it cleaning products?"

"There are similarities," Nunzio agrees.

"But there are some major differences, too."

"Like what?"

"Like the cosmetic pyramids don't break your face or your legs if you try to operate independently," I sez.

"What I was going to say," Nunzio sez, glarin' at me, "was that the cosmetic chains don't supply you with lawyers, much less alibis, if the authorities take offense at your activities... or your tax reports."

"Oh yeah?" I bristles, gettin' a little fed up with Nunzio's know-it-all attitude. "Well the soapsy folks don't whack you if they think you're shortin' them on their take, either!"

"Well what do you expect 'em to do?" he snaps right back at me. "Have 'em arrested?"

"What's with you, Swatter?" Spyder sez, cockin' her head at me. "You sound like you're really down on the Mob."

"He's just a little edgy," Nunzio puts in quick before I can answer myself. "We were having a bit of an argument when you joined us."

"Oh, I'm sorry, she blinks, poppin' to her feet. "I didn't know I was interrupting anything. I can catch you guys later. Just think about what I was asking, okay?"

We watch her walk away, which is a real treat, as feminine company has been notably lackin' since we started our trainin'. Then Nunzio turns to me.

"Okay. What's eating you?"

"The same thing that's been eatin' me since the Boss sent us on this assignment," I sez. "Talkin' about the Mob makes it harder than usual to ignore. Know what I mean?"

"We wasn't assigned, we volunteered."

"We was *asked* to volunteer by the Boss, which for us is the same as bein' ordered."

Nunzio heaves one of his big sighs and droops a little.

"I guess we might as well have this out right now," he grimaces. "You're talking about us being here in Possiltum right?"

"I'm talkin' about us declarin' war on the Mob," I corrects. "Seein' as how we're currently holdin' the bag at ground zero, this is of some concern to me. Sorry, but I tend to get a bit nervous about overwhelmin'-type firepower when it is apt to be directed at me... especially when all we've got is government issue cross-bows... and leather skirts for armor!"

*

If, perhaps, this concern of mine has taken youse by surprise, allow me to enlighten youse, startin' with a brief history lesson. For those of youse already aware of the danger cousin Nunzio and I are in, however, feel free to skip to the next asterisk-type punctuation mark.

Nunzio and me first met the Boss about five books back [*Hit or Myth* (Myth Adventures #4)] when we was assigned to tag along with one of the Mob's mouthpieces whilst he was looking for the same Big Julie we was con-versin' with in the first chapter. To be more precise, he was lookin' for the army which Big Julie was supposed to have been leadin' in a little fund raisin' venture for our organization, and which, accordin' to reports, had disap-peared into thin air after encounterin' a bit of resistance led by the Boss. Of course, in those days we didn't call him the Boss as we weren't workin' for him at the time. All we knew was that there was some bad news-type sorcerer named Skeeve the Great givin' the Mob grief and we was supposed to keep him off Shyster's back whilst the investigation progressed.

In the interest of brevity not to mention the preservin' of our royalty income from the backlist of this series, I will refrain from narratin' all the intriguin' details of that assignment. What is crucial that you understand, however, is that at the conclusion of that first encounter, a deal was struck between the Great Skeeve and Don Bruce, the Mob's Fairy Godfather. By the terms of that agreement, Don Bruce and the Mob was to lay off the Kingdom of Possiltum in general and Big Julie and his boys specifically, in exchange for the Great Skeeve givin' the Mob access to another dimension... to wit, Deva, complete with its rather famous bazaar.

Shortly thereafter, Don Bruce hired the Great Skeeve to oversee the Mob's interests on Deva, and assigned Nunzio and me to him as bodyguards... which is when we started callin' him Boss.

With me so far?

Okay, now review the circumstantials with me again, and see if youse can understand the dilemma facin' us.

First of all, the Boss is working for the Mob.

Second, he has sent us to deal with the situation in Possiltum while he goes after Aahz.

Now, as he works for the Mob and we all work for him, the entire strike force which is currently movin' on Queen Hemlock can be considered to be in the employment of the Mob.

Unfortunately, there is a deal in effect, one personally negotiated by Don Bruce himself, which says that no one in the Mob is to move against Possiltum! This means that our current operation is in direct violation of Don Bruce's sworn word... and while I can't say that notable has never gone back on his word, to do so is a decision he usually reserves for himself personally and tends to get more than a little peeved when someone else undertakes to break his word for him.

As you may have noted from followin' whatever type of media is in vogue where you're readin' this, when someone of Don Bruce's level in the Mob gets peeved, it is not usually expressed by an angry memo. If he feels his position or authority in the Mob is bein' challenged by some overly frisky underling, his usual response is to squash said underling like a bug. Of course, in our position as bodyguards to the Boss, this places us between the Squasher and the Squashee, resultin' in the edginess I was referrin' to a couple pages back which necessitated this explanation.

Understand now? If not, just trust me that I know more about these things than youse, and that our whole crew will be in trouble with the Mob when and if Don Bruce finds out what we're doin'.

*

"I've been giving it a lot of thought," Nunzio sez like he never left the conversation, which of course, he hadn't, "and I'm not sure the Boss *knows* he's crossing Don Bruce by sending us back here."

Now this set me back on my heels a bit. I had been assumin' all along that Skeeve sendin' us here was a premeditated move. The idea that he might be ignorant of the consequentials of this action had never occurred to me.

"How do you figure that?"

"Well, the way I see it, the Boss is a real sharp cookie... except in two areas: the Mob, and broads."

"That's true," I sez, 'cause it was. While I have nothin' but the highest regard for the Boss overall, in those two areas he tends to be what we refer to in the Mob as "dumb as a stone."

"Also," Nunzio continues, "there's the fact that he didn't consult with us about the advisabilities of startin' a ruckus with the Mob, or even warn us to be careful of anything except Hemlock... which is not like him at all if he was expecting trouble from Don Bruce."

Again he has hit on a valid point. Skeeve has easily been the most considerate Boss we have ever worked with, and has always been sensitive to our feelin's... especially those which is attached to parts of us which bleed or break. This has a lot to do with the loyalty and genuine affection we hold for him... along with his pay scale which is both generous and dependable.

"Now that you mention it," I sez, "it wouldn't make much sense for the Boss to get into a power struggle or try to take over from Don Bruce, as he has never expressed any interest in or desire to elevate his standin' in the Mob."

Nunzio shrugged. "If that were his inclination, all he'd have to do is marry Bunny and let Don Bruce hand him the whole organization on a platter as an inheritance."

He is referrin' to the fact that not only is

Bunny Don Bruce's niece, she is head over heels in love with the Boss... somethin' which seems to have escaped his notice entirely. Like we said earlier... The Mob and broads... Stone stupid.

"You may be right..."

"Of course I'm right! It all fits!"

"...But even if you are, I'm not sure what difference it makes," I finish, ignoring his rude interruption. "Whether we're breakin' Don Bruce's word by accident or on purpose, we will still be in the line of fire when that notable decides to put things right."

"The difference is that if we assume the Boss *doesn't* want trouble with Don Bruce, we aren't obligated to stand and fight. More specifically, we're free to try to act as peace-makers between the two of them before blood starts to flow.

This reasonin' has a certain appeal to it, particularly as if said blood does indeed begin to flow, the odds are that it will be the two of us at the source of said flow.

"Okay," I sez. "*Assumin'* that you're right about the Boss not wantin' trouble, and *assumin'* that Don Bruce lets you get a word in edgewise before the shootin' starts, what are you gonna say to cool him down?"

"That part," Nunzio hesitates, "...that part I'm still working on."

It occurs to me that until my cousin comes up with a surefire sales pitch to settle things, all that takin' a peace-maker role is accomplishin' is committin' us not to shoot back when the trouble starts!

Chapter 6

"Boards don't hit back!"
B. Lee

Pre-inhabited as I was with my worries about Don Bruce and the Mob, the altercation between Sergeant Smiley and myself slipped my mind completely. As it turned out, however, this did not matter, as the sergeant took steps to remind me of it, and the way it was sprung on me, it wouldn't have done me no good to have used up a lot of time and energy thinkin' about it

We had reached the portion of our trainin' in which we was to learn how to relate to the enemy at close quarters... preferably without surrenderin'. That is to say, hand-to-hand type combat.

Sergeant Smiley was teachin' this section himself, which did not strike me as odd until later, as he obviously had more than passin' familiarity with the techniques we was to learn. He homed in on the Flie brothers as his demonstrator/victims, and had great fun showin' us all that size was not a factor in hand-to-hand combat by tossin' and punchin' 'em both around with impressive ease... or, put differently, he really made them fly.

While all this was great fun to watch, I could not help thinkin' that the lesson he was attemptin' to drive home stank higher than the "Realistic Doggie Doodle With Lifelike Aroma that Actually Sticks to Your Hands" that I was so familiar with. I mean, I wonder if he really thought he was foolin' anyone with his "size doesn't make a difference" spiel. It doesn't take a genius to figure out that size can make a *considerable* difference in a physical-type difference of opinion, as one honest to goodness fight will usually demonstrate this fact clearly enough to convince even the dimmest of wits. The only time skill triumphs over size is if the little guy is *very* skillful and the big guy is very *unskillful*... not to mention slow and maybe has a glass jaw. If they are at all matched for skill, the big guy is a good bet to make strawberry jam of the little guy if he is so inclined. This is why professional contact, sport-type athletes, not to mention kneecappers like Nunzio and me, are on the extra-large side. It isn't because our employers figure we are cheaper if cost justified on a "by the pound" rate, it's because we tend to win.

Of course, even if one accepts the "skill over size" concept, there is still a glarin' flaw in the sergeant's logic. Remember how long I said it would take to train someone with a longbow?

(No, this isn't gonna be a test... I was just askin'.) Well, it takes even longer to train someone to be skillful at Hand-To-Hand. A *lot* longer. The idea that someone like the Spellin' Bee could absorb enough skill in one afternoon to be effective against one of the Flie brothers, *however* unskilled, is laughable. Realizin' this, it was clear to me that even though he *said* we was bein' prepared for combat with the enemy, all he was doin' was showin' us a few tricks to help us survive the inevitable barroom type brawls which seem to naturally gravitate toward people in uniform who are tryin' to have a quiet drink around civilians durin' their off-duty hours. Simply put, we was bein' trained to deal with unskilled civilian-type fighters, preferably blind staggerin' drunk, rather than against skilled soldier-type fighters in the field.

"*...Of course, these are techniques which will enable you to dispatch an unarmed opponent!*" Sergeant Smiley was sayin', which was again misleadin' as none of the countermoves he was demonstratin' were lethal enough to 'dispatch' anyone, confirmin' my belief that *someone* was figurin' we'd only use them on civilians.

"*...To deal with an ARMED opponent, however, is a different matter entirely! Fortunately, we have an EX-PERT with us to demonstrate how that is done! GUIDO! Front and center!*"

"Me, Sergeant?" I blinks, as I had not expected to be called upon.

"That's right," the sergeant sez, showin' some extra teeth in his smile. "At the firing range you made a big point that only jerks have to kill people. Well, here's your chance to show everybody how to 'gentle' an enemy into submission when he's trying to kill you."

Needless to say, I don't care for the sounds of this, but as I have been summoned, I have little choice but to step forward into the clear space bein' used for the demonstrations. My discomfort grows as the sergeant gestures to Corporal Whittle, who tosses him a short sword. That's right, a real short sword... with a point and sharpened edges.

"What's with the sword, Sergeant?" I sez.

"I *said* this was going to be a demonstration against an armed opponent," he grins. "What we're going to do is I'm going to try to kill you, and you're going to try to stop me without killing me."

"...And if I don't?"

"Then I guess we'll have us a little 'training accident'... unless, of course, you'd rather just back out now and admit you can't do it."

Needless to say, I did not obtain my current lofty position as bodyguard by backin' away from fights. What's more, the sword wasn't my real worry as it is nothin' more than a long knife, and I've dealt with knives often enough.

"Oh, I can do it," I shrugs. "The trouble is it might involve striking a non-commissioned officer... which I seem to recall from our Military Law lesson is a no-no."

The sergeant's smile fades a bit, and I realize he has been expectin' me to withdraw from this exercise when he feeds me the cue. Unfortunately for both of us, this realization comes a little late to do us any good.

"Don't worry about that, 'Cruit,' " he sez, though I notice his voice has gotten tighter. "Even if you get *real* lucky and tag me, you're acting under orders so no charges will be brought."

That was all I needed to hear. As a last precaution, I glance back at Nunzio where he's standin' in line, and he gives me a little nod with his head.

"Your cousin can't help you now, Guido," Smiley snaps, regainin' a bit of confidence. "This is between you and me."

That wasn't why I was checkin' with Nunzio, but I have no trouble goin' with the flow, bein' real adaptable when the music is startin' and I am one of the designated dancers.

"I was just wonderin'," I sez with a shrug. "It's nice to know *you* know I'd be under orders. The question is whether or not that officer knows it."

Now the sergeant is no dummy and I really don't expect him to fall for the old "there's someone behind you" gag... but he does. It isn't until much later that I find out non-coms have a real thing about officers. That is, they are comfortable runnin' the army... unless there is an officer somewhere in witnessin' range. Anyway, Smiley starts cranin' his neck around tryin' to spot the officer to which I am referrin', and when his head is turned away from me, I glide in on him.

If this tactic sounds a little strange to you, realize that if someone waves a sharpened hunk of metal at you, the last thing they are expectin' is for you to charge them. What you are *supposed* to do is freeze up, or better yet run, thereby givin' them ample leisure time to carve their initials on whatever portion of your anatomy is handiest. When you move forward instead of back, it tends to startle them, and they usually react by pokin' at you with their weapon to try to get you to back off like the script says. This is really what you want, as it has put *you* in control of their attack and lets you bring it in where and when you want it instead of just standin' and hopin' they'll go away while they play around on their own time-table.

The sergeant sees me comin' out of the corner of his eye, and, just like I expect, he sticks his sword out like he's hopin' I'll run into it and save him the trouble of havin' to plan and execute an attack of his own. This makes it easy for me to weave past his point and latch onto the wrist of his sword arm with my left hand, which keeps the weapon out of mischief and me, whilst I give him a medium strength pop under the ear with my right fist.

It was my genuine hope that this would end the affair without further waltzin', but the sergeant is still a pretty tough old bird and it only crosses his eyes and drops him to one knee. I realize the situation has just become dangerous, as he still has hold of his sword and in his dazed condition may not remember that this is only an exercise... if that was his original intention at all.

"Give it up, Sarge," I hisses quiet-like, steppin' in close so's only he can hear me. "It's over."

Just to be on the safe side I wind his arm up a little as I am sayin' this to prove my point. Unfortunately, he either doesn't hear me or chooses to ignore what you must admit is excellent advice, and starts strugglin' around tryin' to bring his sword into play.

"Suit yourself," I shrugs, not really expectin' a response, as at that moment he faints, mostly because I have just broken his arm... for safety sake, mind you. (For the squeamish readers, I will hasten to clarify that this is a clean break as opposed to the messier compound variety, and that it probably wouldn't have put the sergeant out if he hadn't been woozy already from the clout I have just laid on him. As I have noted before, *controlled* violence is my specialty... and I'm *very* good at it.)

"WHAT ARE YOU DOING TO..."

These last words come from Corporal Whittle who has come alive far too late and tries to intervene after the dance is already done. The incomplete nature of his question is due to the fact that, as he is steppin' forward, he runs into a high swing from Nunzio's elbow goin' in the opposite direction, which effectively stretches him out on his back and turns his lights out... and also stops his annoyin' prattle. For the record, this is what the earlier exchange between Nunzio and me was all about... my makin' sure he was in position and willin' to cover my back while I dealt with the sergeant.

There is a moment's silence, then someone in the ranks lets out a low, surprised whistle, which seems to cue everyone to put in their two cents worth.

"Wow!"

"Nice goin', Swatter!!"

" 'Bout time someone taught him to..."

Hy Flie starts nudgin' the corporal's nappin' form with his toe.

"They don't look so big lying down, do they, Swatter?" he grins, like he took the two of 'em out all by himself.

79

"AT EASE! ALL OF YOUSE!!" I bellows, cuttin' the discussion off short. "If you touch that man again, Hy, you and I are gonna go a couple rounds. YOU UNNERSTAND ME??"

He looks surprised and hurt, but nods his agreement.

"I can't hear you!!!"

"YES, SAR... I mean, GUIDO!!"

"THAT GOES FOR THE REST OF YOUSE TOO!" I snarls. "I DON'T WANT TO SEE YOU KICKIN' EITHER OF THESE TWO, *OR* MAKIN' FUN OF THEM *UNLESS* YOU'RE WILLIN' TO DO THE SAME THING WHEN THEY'RE AWAKE AND ABLE TO HIT BACK. *DO I MAKE MYSELF CLEAR??"*

"YES, GUIDO!!!"

As might be noticed in my manner, I am a bit annoyed at this point, but mostly with myself. I am genuinely irked that I was unable to squelch the sergeant's move without havin' to break his arm, and am quite willin' to take my anger out on the crew. If my speech pattern when addressin' my colleagues seems uncharacteristic, it is because I discovered quickly that the army's non-coms have a point... it *is* the easiest way to shout at an entire formation at the same time.

"Okay, now LISTEN UP!! As Actin' Squad Leader, I am the rankin' individual present until such time as the sergeant and corporal regain consciousness. I want one volunteer to get a medic for these two, while the REST OF US CONTINUE WITH THE TRAININ' EXERCISE!!

This strikes me as the logical course to follow, as I am not eager to lose a day's trainin' whilst waitin' for our non-coms to wake up. At this point, however, I notice my cousin has raised his hand politely for my attention.

"Yes, Nunzio? Are you volunteerin' to go for a medic?"

"Not really, *Acting Squad Leader* Guido, sir," he sez, sarcastic-like. "I was just thinking that, before you assumed command, it might be wise for you to check in with the officer over there who *is* the ranking individual present."

Now, as youse will recall, when I pulled this gag on the sergeant, it was a ploy to divert his attention. I've played Dragon Poker with Nunzio though, and I can tell when he's bluffin'... and this time he wasn't. With a sinkin' feelin' in my stomach, I turn to look in the direction he is pointin'. Sure enough, there is an officer there, the first I have seen outside of our lectures. What is worse, he is comin' our way with a real grim look on his face.

*

"Stand easy, Guido."

I switch from Attention to At Ease, which is not to say I am at ease at all. I have been summoned to the Officers' Tent, which is not surprisin' as it is obvious I am gonna take some kinda flack for the afternoon's skirmish. What does take me off guard is that Sergeant Smiley is there as well, sportin' a sling for his arm and a deadpan expression.

"Sergeant Smiley here has given me his version of what's been going on with your training group that led up to the event I witnessed this afternoon. Would you like to tell me your side of the story?"

I'm sure the sergeant's account is complete and accurate... sir." I sez, crisp-like.

Normally, I would have just clammed up until I had a lawyer, but so far no charges have been mentioned, and I somehow don't think this is a good time to make waves.

"Very well," the officer nods. "In that case I feel compelled to follow the sergeant's recommendation in this case."

It occurs to me that maybe I should have offered up some defense, but it is too late now, as the officer has already swung into action. Pickin' up a quill, he scribbles his name across the bottom of a series of papers that have been sittin' on his desk.

"Do you know what an army that's been growing as fast as ours needs the most, Guido?" he sez as he's writin'.

I start to say "Divine Intervention," but decide to keep my mouth shut... which is just as well as he proceeds to answer his own question.

"Leadership," he sez, finishin' his signin' with a flourish of his quill. "We're always on the lookout for new leaders... which is why I'm so pleased to sign these orders."

For a change, I have no difficulty lookin' innocent and dumb, as he has totally lost me with his train of thought.

"Sir?"

"What I have here are the papers promoting you to sergeant and Nunzio... he's your cousin, isn't he?... to corporal."

Now I am really lost.

"Promotions, sir?"

"That's right. Sergeant Smiley here has told me how the two of you have taken it on yourselves to lead your squad during training... even to the point of giving them extra training during off duty hours. After seeing for myself how you took command after... that mishap

82

during training today, I have no problem approving your promotion. That's the kind of leadership and incentive we like to see here in the army. Congratulations."

"Thank you, sir," I sez, not bein' able to think of anything else to say.

"Oh yes... and one other thing. I'm pulling your entire unit out of training and assigning them to active duty. It's only garrison duty, but it's the only thing available right now. I figure that anything more they need to learn, you can help them pick up on the job. That's all... Sergeant Guido."

It takes me a minute to register he is addressin' me by my new rank, but I manage to come to attention and salute before turnin' to go.

"If I may, sir," I heard Sergeant Smiley say, "I'd like to have a word outside with Sergeant Guido before he rejoins his unit."

I am half-expectin' Smiley to try to jump me, bad arm and all, once we get outside, or at least lay some heavy threats on me about what would happen the next time our paths cross. Instead, he is all grins and holds out his good hand for me to shake.

"Congratulations, Guido... sorry, I mean *Sergeant* Guido," he sez. "There was one thing I wanted to say to you away from the other recruits."

"What's that, Sergeant?"

"I wanted to ell you that you were right all along... it *does* take more skill to handle a combat situation without killing... and I'm glad to see we're getting men of your abilities enlisting on our side. Just remember, though, that we only have limited time to train the recruits...

which is why we focus on getting them to think in terms of 'kills." If they're at all squeamish about killing, if they think they can get by by disarming the enemy, they'll try to do that instead... and they don't have the skill and we don't have the time to teach it to them, so they end up dead themselves and we end up placing second in a two army fight. Try to keep that in mind the next time you're working with a group of raw recruits. In the meantime, good luck! Maybe we'll get a chance to serve together again sometime."

I am so surprised by the sergeant turnin' out to be a good Joe, not to mention givin' careful consideration to the thoughts he laid on me, that I am nearly back to the unit before the full impact of my promotion sinks in.

Then, I feel depressed. My entire career has been geared toward avoidin' bein' an authority-type figure, and now I am saddled with what is at least a supervisory post... permanent this time instead of temporary. My only consolations are that a) I can potentially do more damage havin' a higher rank, and b) Nunzio has to suffer the burden of extra stripes right along with me.

Perkin' up a little from these thoughts, I go lookin' for Nunzio, wantin' to be the first to slip him the bad news.

Chapter 7

"To Serve and Protect..."
**traditional motto of
protection rackets**

As eager as we are to get on with our assignment, which is to say demoralizin' and disruptin' the army, both Nunzio and me are more than a little nervous about doin' garrison duty.

Not that there is anything wrong with the town, mind you. Twixt is a bigger'n average military town, which means there is lots of stuff to keep us amused during our off-duty hours. The very fact that it is a sizable burg, however, increases the odds of our presence bein' noticed and reported to Don Bruce... which, as we have mentioned before, was not high on our list of desirable occurrences.

The duty itself was annoyin'ly easy, annoyin' in that it's hard to stir up the troops when the worst thing facin' them is boredom. The situation is readily apparent even when I put Nunzio to work settlin' our crew in whilst I report in to the garrison commander.

"Our only real job here is to maintain a military presence... show the flag so's folks remember why they're paying their taxes."

The individual deliverin' this speech is average height, about a head shorter than me, and has dark tight-curly hair with a few wisps of grey showin' in spots... which might have made him look dignified if he didn't move like a dock worker tryin' to finish early so's he can go on a heavy date. He has a rapid-fire kinda speech pattern and rattles off his orders without lookin' up from the papers he is scribblin' on. I can't help but notice, however, that what he is workin' on so hard looks a lot like poetry... which I somehow don't think is covered by his official orders.

"All you and your boys gotta do is spend a certain number of hours a day patrolling the streets in uniform so's folks can see the army is here. The rest of the time, you're on your own."

"You mean like *policemen?*"

The words just sorta popped outta my mouth, but they must'a had a note of horror in them, as the commander broke off what he was doin' to look at me direct.

"Not really," he sez, quick like. "We used to be responsible for patrolling the streets, but the town's grown to a point where it has its own police force, and we try not to interfere with their authority. They watch the citizens, and our own Military Police watches our troops. Clear and separate. See?"

86

"Yes sir."

"...which brings us to another point," the commander continues, startin' to scribble on his papers again. "There's a non-fraternization rule in effect for our troops. We don't enforce it too strictly, so you don't have to worry if one of the... ah, ladies makes advances toward you or your men, but let them come to you. Don't start messing around with the ordinary civilian women. It's liable to get the civilian *men* upset however it goes, and our main directive here is to *not* incite any trouble with the civilians. Be nice to them... show them we're just plain folks, like they are. If you can do that, then they're less inclined to believe any wild stories they might hear about what our troops are doing on the front lines. Got that?"

I didn't think it would really matter what I said or did, as the commander is rattlin' all this off like it is memorized while he fiddles with his writin'. I didn't think it would be wise to test this theory, however.

"Yes sir," I sez. "No fraternizin' with the women... No fightin' with the men. Got it."

"Very well, report back to your unit and see that they're properly settled in. Then take the rest of the day to familiarize yourselves with the town, and report here for assignment to-morrow morning."

"Yes sir." I draw myself up and give him a snappy salute, which he returns without even lookin' up.

I can't help but feel I have kinda gotten the bum's rush on my briefin', so on the way out I pause to have few words with the commander's clerk... a decision which I'll admit is in part due to the factual that she is the only skirt I have seen in uniform except for Spyder, and I am beginnin' to feel a little desperate for the sound of a female-type voice. Besides, I outrank her, and figure it is about time my new stripes work a little *for* me instead of against me.

"What's the deal with the commander?" I sez, friendly-like, givin' her one of my lesser used non-intimidatin' smiles.

Instead of respondin', however, this chick just stares at me blankly like she's still waitin' for me to say somethin'. Now, she is a tiny little thing, a bit on the slender side, so her starin' at me with those big eyes of hers starts makin' me feel a little uncomfortable... like she's a praying mantis tryin' to decide if she should eat me before or after we mate.

"I mean, how come he's writin' poetry?" I add, just to get some kinda conversation flowin'.

"Lyrics," she sez, in a flat sort of voice.

"Excuse me?"

"I said 'lyrics'... as in 'words for songs.' He likes to perform in the local clubs at their open stage nights, and he writes his own material... constantly."

"Is he any good?"

This gets me a small shrug.

"I suppose he's not bad... but he doesn't play guitar, so mostly he has to sing a cappella. That makes his performance sound a little thin after listening to an evening of singers with instrumental accompaniments."

I notice that for all her apparent disinterest, this chick seems to know a lot about what the commander does on his off hours... even to the point of sittin' through a whole evenin' of amateur singers to listen to his set when she doesn't really like his singin'. From this I deduce that I am not likely to get much of anywhere with her as a sergeant, so I settle for bein' friendly.

"Maybe he should try keyboards," I sez.

"Try what?" she blinks, suddenly takin' more interest in the conversation.

"Key... Oh! Nothin'. Hey, I got to be goin' now. Nice talkin' with you."

With that I beat a hasty retreat, a little annoyed with myself. Again my time on Deva has almost gotten me in trouble. For a second there, I forgot that this dimension not only doesn't have keyboards, it does not have the electricity necessary for the pluggin' in of said instrument.

"Hey Guido!" comes a familiar voice, interruptin' my thoughts. "What's the word?"

I look around to find Nunzio and the rest of the crew bearin' down on me.

"No big deal," I shrugs. "We don't even go on duty until tomorrow. The commander's given us the rest of the day off to settle in and check out the town."

"Sounds good to me," Hy Flie sez, rubbin' his hands together like... well, like a fly. "What say we get something to eat... and at the same time see if we can find a place to hang out on our off-duty hours."

"How about the spaghetti place we passed on the way here?" Spyder sez, jerkin' her head back in the direction they had come from.

I shoot a quick glance at Nunzio, who is already lookin' at me. As so often happens when we're workin' together, we are thinkin' the same thing at the same time, and this time we're both thinkin' that the best way to avoid runnin' into someone with Mob connections is by *not* usin' a spaghetti place for a base of operations.

"Ah... let's see if we can find someplace less likely... I mean, *closer*." I suggest, casual-like.

"Well, how 'bout we try right here?" Nunzio chimes in, pickin' up on my general train of thought.

I look where he is pointin', and have to admit that it is probably the last place someone from the Mob would think of lookin' for us. The sign over the door of the joint reads, ABDUL'S SUSHI BAR AND BAIT SHOP.

"Sushi?" Shu Flie scowls, "You mean like raw fish?"

"At least we know it's fresh," Junebug sez, gesturin' at the second part of the sign.

"Oh, don't be a bunch of babies!" Spyder grins, givin' Shu a poke in the ribs. "Wait 'til you've tried it. It's good! Come on."

Now, I am no more enthusiastic than the Flie brothers about eatin' this stuff, even though Nunzio has been after me for some time to give it a try. I mean, I'm used to fish in a tomato sauce or somethin', served with pasta-- not rice. Still, there seems little option than to follow Spyder and Nunzio as they merrily lead the way into the place.

"Ah! Members of our noble fighting forces!" the proprietor sez, slitherin' up out of the dim depths to greet us. "Please, come right in. We give special discounts for our men... and ladies... in uniform!"

"Can we have a table close to the window so's there's more light?" Nunzio sez, givin' me a wink.

I know what he is thinkin' and normally

90

would approve. The proprietor is makin' me feel a little uneasy, however. Despite his toothy smile, I have a strong feelin' he can tell within a few pieces of small change how much money our crew is carryin'... and is already tryin' to figure how much of it he can glom onto before we escape. In short, I haven't felt this sized up by a merchant since we left the Bazaar at Deva.

Despite my growin' discomfort, I join the crew as the proprietor ushers us to a window table and distributes menus. Everybody gives their drink orders, then start porin' over the menus with Spyder and Junebug servin' as interpreters... everyone except Nunzio, that is.

Ignorin' his menu completely, my cousin starts fishin' around in his belt pouch.

"While we're here, anyone care for a couple quick hands of Dragon Poker?" he sez innocent like, producin' a deck of cards and a battered, dog-eared book.

The whole crew groans at this, a sure indication of their familiarity with the game, which is not surprisin' as Nunzio and me have been takin' great pains to teach it to 'em. Despite their apparent reluctance, however, I notice that their stakes money appears on the table in a quick ripple of movement, which is in itself a testimony to the addictin' nature of this particular pastime. I can speak from my own experience in sayin' that there is nothin' like watchin' a pot you've built on a nice hand disappear into someone else's stack because of some obscure type Conditional Modifier to convince a new player that it is definitely in his best interest to learn more about the game as it is his only chance of winnin' some of his money back, much less show a profit. That is, you play your first game of Dragon Poker for the fun of it, and after that youse is playin' for revenge.

"Okay... ante up!" Nunzio sez, givin' the cards a quick shuffle and offerin' the deck for a cut.

"Not so fast, cousin," I interrupts, fishin' my own copy of the rulebook out. "First, let's settle what the Conditional Modifiers are."

"Why bother?" Shu Flie grimaces. "They change every day."

"Every day? You mean every hour!" his brother sez.

"Whatever," Spyder shrugs. "Start dealing Nunzio. Swatter here can fill us in on the high points."

For those of youse unfamiliar with Dragon Poker, it is a very popular means of redistrib-utin' wealth throughout the dimensions. You can think of it as nine card stud poker with six card hands... that is, if you don't mind gettin' your brains beat out financially. You see, on top of the normal rules of card playin', there are Conditional Modifiers which can change the value of a card or hand dependin' on the di-mension, hour of the day, number of players, position at the table, or any one of a multitude of other factors, makin' Dragon Poker the most difficult and confusin' card game in all the di-mensions.

Nunzio and me got fascinated by dis game whilst everyone was tryin' to teach it to the Boss in time for his big match with the Sen-Sen Ante Kid, and it isn't really all that hard... providin' one has a copy of the rules applicable to the dimension youse is in at the time. (Of course, the Boss couldn't use a book durin' the big match, as he was supposed to be an expert already.) Before leavin' the Bazaar for this particular caper, both Nunzio and me included pickin' up copies of the rulebook for Klah (our home dimension where dis narration is takin' place) as part of our preparations. If youse, perhaps think that buyin' two copies of the rulebook is a needless expense, let me give youse a free tip about playin' Dragon Poker: Your best defense at the table is havin' your own copy of the rules. Youse see, one of the standin' rules in *any* Dragon Poker game is that the players are individually responsible for knowin' the Conditional Modifiers. Put simply, this means that if you don't know a particular modifier which would turn your nothin' hand into a winner, no one is obligated to announce it to you. This is a tradition of the game and has nothin' to do with the honesty of them what plays it. If anything, it avoids accusations that a player deliberately withheld information to win a hand rather than a particular modifier simply bein' overlooked amidst the multitude of modifiers in effect at any given time. In short, as much as I trust my cousin Nunzio to cover my back in a brawl, I feel it wisest *not* to count on him lookin' out for my interests at a Dragon Poker table, and therefore figure havin' my own copy of the rulebook is a necessary expense, not a luxury or convenience.

"Let's see," I sez, thumbin' through the book, "the sun is out... and we're playin' indoors..."

"...and there's an odd number of players..." Spyder supplies, showin' she's gettin' the hang of the modifyin' factors.

"...and one of them is female... sort of..."

Junebug adds, winkin' at Spyder.

"Sorry to take so long with your drinks, my friends," the proprietor sez, announcin' his presence as he arrives back at the table with a tray of potables. "Now, who has the... *HEY! WHAT IS THIS???!!!*"

It suddenly occurs to me that there may be some local ordinance against gamblin'... which would explain why the proprietor is suddenly so upset.

"This? I sez, innocent-like. "Oh, we're just havin' a friendly little game of cards here. Don't worry, we're just usin' the coins to keep score and..."

"Don't give me that!" our host snarls, with no trace of his earlier greasy friendliness. "That's Dragon Poker you're playing! No one plays that game unless..."

He breaks off sudden-like and starts givin' each of us the hairy eyeball.

"All right, which one of you is a demon? Or is it all of you? Never mind! I want you all out of here... *RIGHT NOW!!!*"

Chapter 8

"It takes one to know one!"
Jack D. Ripper

To say the proprietor's accusation caused a stir at our table is like sayin' it would cause raised eyebrows to have Don Bruce as the guest speaker at a Policeman's Banquet. Unfortuitously, everyone had different questions to ask.

"What's he mean 'demon'?" Spyder demanded.

I started to answer her, as I knew from my work with the Boss that a demon is the commonly accepted term for a dimension traveler, but there was too much cross-talk for rational-type conversation.

"Are we supposed to leave?" Spellin' Bee sez, scared-like as he peered at the retreatin' figure.

"What's wrong with Dragon Poker?" Shu Flie put in.

"Nothin'," I sez to him. "You see, Spyder..."

"Then what put the burr under his saddle?" Shu pressed, startin' to get under my skin.

Fortunately, in trainin' I have discovered there is one way to shut this particular individual up when he gets on a roll.

"Shu Flie," I sez, "don't bother me."

It was an old joke by this time, but it still got a laugh... which is not surprisin' as I have found that the vast majority of army humor pivots on old jokes.

"Watch yourself, brother," Hy Flie sez, pokin' Shu in the ribs. "The Swatter there is lookin' to squash a fly again... and he might not be too picky about which of us he swats."

Under the cover of this new round of laughs, Nunzio leans forward to talk to me direct.

"Are you thinking what I'm thinking, cuz?"

"That, of course, depends upon what it is you are thinkin', Nunzio," I sez, reasonable-like. "If, perchance, you are thinkin' that you can color our cover 'blown,' then we are, indeed, thinkin' along the same lines."

To my surprise, instead of agreein' he rolls his eyes like he does when I'm missin' something which to him is obvious.

"Think it through, Guido," he sez. "He thinks we're from off-dimension, because we know about Dragon Poker... right?"

"Yeah. So?"

"So how does *he* know about it?"

To me, this question is as trivial as wonderin' how a cop happens to know about a particular ordinance... which is to say it is beside the point, totally overlookin' the immediate dilemma of dealin' with the aftermath of us gettin' caught breakin' it.

"I dunno. I guess someone showed it to him. So what?"

For some reason, this seems to get Nunzio even more upset.

"Guido," he sez, clenchin' his teeth, "sometimes I wonder if all those knocks on the head you've taken have... oops! He's coming back. Quick... Bee?"

"Yes, Nunzio?" our junior magician sez, blinkin' with surprise at havin' been suddenly included in our discussion.

"Get your Dis-spell ready, and when I give you the nod... throw it on the proprietor."

"The proprietor? Why?"

"Bee... just do it. Okay?" I interrupts, havin' learned from experience that the only thing that takes longer than listenin' to one of Nunzio's lectures is tryin' to pry a straight answer out of him when he's tryin' to let you discover the point yourself.

Bee starts to say somethin', then shuts his mouth, shrugs, startin' to mumble and mutter like he does when he's gettin' ready to use magik.

The others at the table look at Nunzio expectant-like, but he just leans back in his chair lookin' confident and smug. I, of course, imitate his action, though I have no more idea what he is about to pull than the rest of the crew. You see, past experience has taught me that one of the best times to act confident is when youse is totally in the dark... but would just as soon no one else is aware of your ignorance.

"Are you still here?" the proprietor demands, materializin' beside our table again. "I don't want to have to tell you again! Now get out before I call the cops!"

"I don't think so," Nunzio sez, starin' at the ceilin'.

"WHAT??!!"

"...In fact, I was thinkin' we might want to make your place our home away from home... If you know what I mean."

"Izzat so?! Think just 'cause you're in the Army you can do anything you want, do you? Well, let me tell you something, soldier-boy. I happen to be a tax paying member of this community in good standing with the authorities, and soldiers or not they don't take too kindly to demons in these parts. In fact, I can't think of one good reason why I shouldn't call the police right now and have them drag you all right out of here!"

"I can," Nunzio smiles, and nods at Bee.

At the cue, Spellin' Bee squares his shoulders, purses his lips, and lets fly with his Dis-Spell, and...

"*What the...*"

"*MY GOD!!!*"

"*Lookit...*"

The reason for this outpourin' of surprise and disbelief on the part of our crew is that, despite our time with them, Nunzio and me has failed to brief or otherwise prepare them for acceptin' the concept of demons... which is what they're suddenly confronted with. That is, as soon as Bee completed his spell, there was a ripplin' in the air around the proprietor, and instead of a greasy local type, he now looked just like...

"A Deveel!" I sez, hidin' my own surprise.

Actually, I am a little annoyed at myself for not havin' figured it out on my own. I mean, no matter what he looked like, I had been thinkin' that he was actin' like a Deveel since I first set eyes on him.

The reaction of our crew to this discovery, however, is nothin' compared to the reaction we gets from the proprietor.

"WHAT ARE YOU DOING!!??" he screeches, lookin' around the place desperately, only to find we are the only ones present. *"YOU TRYIN' TO GET ME LYNCHED???"*

With that, he goes scuttlin' off, leavin' Nunzio and me to deal with the confusion caused by the removal of his disguise.

"THAT WAS A DEVIL!!!"

I miss who exactly it is who observes this particular utterance, as it is said behind me and the choked, gargley nature of the voice makes positive identification no easy task. Still, I have no difficulty comin' up with a response.

"I know. That's was I said before," I explain.

"No, you said he was a Da-veel," Junebug sez frownin'.

"Same difference," I shrugs.

"Look," Spyder sez, holdin' up a hand to the others for them to be quiet. "Are you guys going to tell us what's goin' on here or not?"

"Guido," Nunzio sez, jerkin' his head in the direction the proprietor has gone. "Why don't you go do a little negotiating with our host before he gets *too* recovered from our little surprise, whilst I try to explain the facts of life to our colleagues."

This is fine by me, as I do not share my

cousin's love of lengthy and confusin' explanations and am glad to be excused from what promises to be a classic opportunity for him to pontificate. Besides, it is not often that one has a chance to really stick it to a Deveel, and as in those few occasions I have been present for, I have usually had rank pulled on my by the financial types of the M.Y.T.H. Inc. team, I am lookin' forward to a rare opportunity to demonstrate my own negotiatin' talents. Of course, it occurs to me that the only witness I will have for this exercise will be the individual upon whom I am turnin' the screws, and he will doubtless be less than appreciative of my finesse. Doin' one's best work in the absence of witnesses is, however, one of the unfortunate and unjust realities of my chosen profession, and I have long since resigned myself to the burden of anonymity... tellin' myself that if I had wanted to be a *well-known* crook, I should have gone into politics.

The proprietor has vanished like a cat burglar at the sound of a bell, but I soon discover him in a small office behind the bar. He is holdin' one of those small foldin' cases with a mirror in it like broads use to check their makeup, only instead of powder and colored goop, his just seems to have a couple dials in it. Starin' into the mirror, he twiddles with the dials a bit... and slowly the disguise he was wearin' before came into focus again, leadin' me to conclude that it is some kind of magik device. If it seems to youse that it took me a long time to reach this conclusion, you are makin' the mistake of underestimatin' my speed of thinkin'. Included in my observational analysis was a certain amount of speculation of whether such a device might be handy to have for my own use... as well as whether it would be better to obtain one on my own or simply include this one in my negotiations.

Apparently the gizmo also functions as a normal mirror, as the proprietor suddenly shifts the angle he is holdin' it at so's we are starin' at each other in the glass, then he snaps it shut and turns to face me.

"What do *you* want?!" he snarls. "Haven't you done enough to me already?"

I do not even bother tryin' to point out that I am not the one what stripped him of his disguise spell, as I have learned durin' my residence on Deva that unless they are actively sellin', which fortunately is most of the time, Deveels are extremely unpleasant and unreasonable folks who do not accept that simple logic is sufficient reason to stop complainin'. They *do* however, respond to reason.

"I have come as a peace emissary," I sez, "in an effort to reach an equitable settlement of our differences."

The Deveel simply makes a rude noise at this, which I magnanimously ignore as I continue.

"I would suggest you meet our offer with equal enthusiasm for peace... seein' as how continued hostilities between us will doubtless result in my colleagues and me trashin' this fine establishment of yours..."

"What? My place?" the proprietor blinks, his mouth continuin' to open and close like a fish out of water.

"...As well as spreadin' the word about your bein' a Deveel to the authorities you was so ungraciously threatenin' us with... and anyone else in this town who will listen. Know what I mean?"

Now, I have this joker cold, and we both know it. Still he rallies back like a punch-drunk boxing champ on the downslide, fightin' more from guts and habit than from any hope of winnin'.

"You can't do that!" he sez, gettin' his mouth workin' well enough to at least sputter. "If you turn me in as a demon, then I'll incriminate you, too! We'll *all* end up getting killed, or at least run out of town."

"There is one major difference in our circumstantials which you are overlookin'," I sez, grinnin' at him. "While I will admit that my cousin and me have done some dimension travelin', this particular dimension of Klah happens to be our home territory. The appearances you see are legit and not disguises, so any attempt to accuse us of bein' from off-dimension would be difficult to prove, as we are not. On the other hand, *you*, bereft of disguise, would encounter extreme difficulty in convincin' a jury or lynch mob that you was from around here."

I thought this would bring any resistance on the proprietor's part to an end, but instead he straightens up and frowns, his eyes takin' on a mean glitter.

"You're from this dimension? You wouldn't happen to know a local magician and demon by the name of *Skeeve*, would you?"

As I have said before, I have not reached my current age and position by panicking under cross-type examination *or* by overratin' the necessity for voicin' the *whole* truth. I can see that this Deveel has some kind of grudge against the Boss, so while habitually avoidin'

103

any false statement which could lead to perjury charges, I am careful not to acknowledge my actual relationship with the individual in question.

"Skeeve?" I sez, frownin' dramatically like I learned to do in theater, "I think I may have heard the name while I was workin' at the Bazaar, but I ain't heard it recently."

"Too bad," the Deveel mutters, almost to himself. "I owe that Klahd a bad turn or two. I spent a couple of years as a statue under a cloud of pigeons because of him. In fact I'd still be there if it weren't for... but that's another story, if you know what I mean."

Of course, from workin' with the Boss, I knew *exactly* what he meant... that the story of his escape was gonna be marketed separately sometime as a short story to generate additional revenue whilst promotin' these books at the same time. Of course, admittin' this understandin' would have been a dead giveaway, so I decide to change the subject instead.

"Yeah, sure. Say, speakin' of names, what's yours, anyway? I mean your *real* name, not this Abdul alias."

"What? Oh! It's Frumple... or it used to be back when I was welcome in my own dimension of Deva."

That had a familiar sound to it, but I decide enough is enough, and take a firm grip on the subject at hand.

"Well, I'm Guido and my cousin what was talkin' to you back at the table is Nunzio... and I believe we was discussin' the terms of our peaceful coexistence with youse?"

Frumple cocked his head to one side, studyin' me close-like.

"You know," he sez, "you sound like you work for the Mob. In fact, now that I think about it, I seem to recall hearing something about the Mob trying to move in on the Bazaar."

"Yeah? So?"

"So I'm already making yearly protection payments to the Mob, and I don't see why I should stand for being shaken down for anything extra."

This information that the Mob is operatin' in these parts is disquietin' to say the least, but I manage not to show any surprise or nervousness.

"Really?" I sez. "Tell me, does your local Mob sales rep know that you're a Deveel?"

"Okay, Okay! I get the point," Frumple says, throwin' up his hands. "What do you want to keep *that* information quiet?"

"Well, since we're lookin' to make this our hangout for a while, I figure we can protect your little secret as a courtesy."

"Really?"

"Sure," I smiles. "Of course, in return, it would be nice if you extended the hospitality of your establishment to us and our friends... as a courtesy."

"I see," he sez, tightenin' his lips to a crooked line. "All right, I guess I don't have much choice. It'll be cheaper to give you free drinks than to have to relocate and start building a business up from scratch. I'll give you free drinks, and maybe an occasional meal. The rooms upstairs are out, though. If I start letting you use those for free, I'll go out of business anyway. They're the profit margin that keeps this place afloat."

"Rooms?"

"Yeah. I've got a few rooms upstairs that I rent to the customers by the hour so they can... have some privacy with any interesting people they happen to meet here. You see, this place gets pretty lively evenings. It's one of the more popular singles bars in town."

"You mean you got broads workin' the joint at night?"

"Certainly not! The women who hang out here have regular high- paying jobs and wouldn't dream of charging for their company."

"So the customers pay you for the rooms, but not the broads," I sez. "Sounds like a sweet setup to me."

"Not *that* sweet," Frumple amends, hastily. "Still, it helps pay the rent."

"Okay. I think we can settle for drinks and food," I shrugs. "Come on out front, Frumple, and I'll let you buy me a drink to show there's no hard feelin's."

"You're too kind," the Deveel grumbles, but he follows me out of the office.

"I think champagne would be appropriate to seal our agreement, don't you?" I sez. "White champagne."

"White champagne?"

"Of course," I smiles, glad for a chance to show off my knowledge and culture. "This here is a sushi bar, ain't it? You think I don't know what color champagne to have with fish?"

Chapter 9

"Manners are acquired, not inherited!"
S. Penn

Things are pretty sweet for a while after I make our arrangement with Frumple. The reduced costs of our off-hour drinkin' are a real boon on the scut wages the army is payin' us, and the Deveel sure had the right of it when he said his sushi bar was a happy huntin' grounds when it came to broads.

Of course, 'broads' is perhaps a mis-nomenclature for the type of women what hang out at this establishment evenings. These was not the usual gum-snappin, vacant-eyed skirts we are used to associatin' with, but rather the classy, fashion-wise young female executive with a lot on the ball what normally wouldn't give lunks like us the time of day. It seems that once we invaded the sanctuary of these upwardly mobile females, however, they was open-minded enough to give us serious consideration in their own deliberations. While I will not try to comment on which of these two types of females actually makes for better companions, there are things to be said for each... though not all those things are complimentary.

There are two flies which mar our enjoyment of this ointment, however, and here I am not referrin' to the Flie brothers. First, there is the ever present danger of runnin' into someone from the Mob, as Frumple's comments have confirmed our suspicion that they maintain some kind of presence here. Second, there is the annoyin' detail that we are supposed to be working on an assignment, not havin' a good time. Naturally, this is the subject of no small amount of conversation between Nunzio and me.

"The trouble is, we can't really do a good job of disruptin' without movin' around town," I was sayin' durin' one such discussion, "and if we move around town, then the odds of our runnin' into someone from the Mob goes way up!"

"Then we'll have to see what we can stir up from right here," my cousin sez. "When you stop to think about it, this is a pretty good setup for it... makin' trouble, I mean. Most of these women have husbands at home, and even the ones that don't have sufficient standing in the community that if it comes to an altercation, the local authorities will have to take her side of it."

"Why do you say that? I mean, why should messin' with *these* broads cause any more hassle than any others?"

Instead of answerin' right away, Nunzio leans back and gives me the hairy eyeball for a few minutes.

"Guido," he says at last, "Are you tryin' to be stupid just to get a rise out of me?"

"What do you mean?"

"I mean that you yourself said that our commander told us that it was okay if we messed with bimbos, but to leave the respectable women alone. Yet now that I am tryin' to put together a specific course of action, you are actin' like it is a brand new concept to you."

"It just seems to me that it is a revoltin' form of class bias and bigotry," I sez, "assumin' that a woman's respectability is a matter of her financial standin' and education. Wouldn't it be better if it were the other way around? I mean, if a woman's respectability determined where she stood in the financial order instead of the other way around?"

"There are two problems with that," Nunzio sez. "First of all, the same unfair standard is applied to men as well... meanin' it holds for everyone, not just women. Them what is rich and educated is always deemed more respectable... if for no other reason than they wield more power and pay more taxes."

"That's true," I sez, noddin' thoughtful like.

"The second problem is that it's completely off the subject of what we was discussion'... which is to say how to cause disruption."

"It is?"

"What is more, any time you try to start a philosophical discussion with me, it is to be taken as a sure sign that you are deliberately tryin' to divert my attention... as normally you avoid such conversations like a subpoena."

109

I say nothin' when he pauses, as he seems to have me cold. I *had* been tryin' to change the subject.

"All of this, the attempt at stupidity and the lame effort at philosophical discussion, leads me to believe that for some reason you are stalling and do not wish to commence working on our assignment. Am I right?"

I avoid his eyes and shrug kinda vague like.

"Come on, Cuz, talk to me," Nunzio urges. "Are you really havin' so much fun playing soldier that you want to prolong the experience?"

"That is not only silly, it is insultin'!" I sez, my annoyance overcomin' my embarrassment at havin' been caught.

"Then what is it? ...If you don't mind my asking?"

"Well... to be honest with youse, Nunzio, I feel a little funny stirrin' up trouble at this particular location, seein' as how it was me what did the negotiatin' with Frumple to not cause him any grief."

Nunzio throws back his head and gives a bark of laughter... which to me is a dubious way to express his sympathy at my plight.

"Let me get this straight," he sez. "You're worrying about dealing fair with a Deveel?"

"You may laugh," I sez, "though I suggest you not do it often when I am the subject of your amusement. Allow me to remind youse, however, that even though Deveels are notoriously hard bargainers, it is also true that once a deal has been struck, they are equally scrupulous about stickin' to the letter of said agreement. As such, it occurs to me that failin' to honor one's own end of such an agreement is

110

to place oneself in a position of bein' even less trustworthy than a Deveel... which is not a label I relish hangin' upon myself."

"Okay... let's examine the letter of said agreement," Nunzio shrugs. "What you agreed to was that we would neither trash his establishment, nor would we reveal the true nature of his identity as a Deveel. Correct?"

"Well... yeah."

"...Neither of which conditions is broken by us directing our attentions to the lovelies which have taken to making this establishment their after-hours habitat... even if our attentions should turn out to be unwelcome."

"I suppose... but don't you think that such activity would violate at least the spirit of our agreement, by which I mean the implication that we would not make trouble for our host?

"That is the portion of your discomfort which I find the most amusing." Nunzio sez with an infuriatin' grin. "Realizing that Deveels make their living as well as their reputation by honoring the letter rather than the spirit of their agreements, I think it is ironic that you are recoiling from dealing with them with the same ethic that they deal with others."

I consider this for a few minutes, then take a deep breath and blow it out noisily.

"You know cousin," I sez. "You're right. I mean, when you're right, you're right... know what I mean?"

"I do," Nunzio frowned, "which is in itself a little disturbing."

"So... when do you think we should start?"

"Well... how about right now?"

While my cousin has convinced me that it would be within the bounds of ethical behavior to launch our campaign, such an accelerated-type timetable catches me unawares.

"Excuse me?"

"I said how about starting right now. Opportunity should be seized when it presents itself... and right now there is a young lady at the bar who has been checking you out for the last several minutes."

I sneak a peek in the direction he is lookin', and sure enough... there is one of those classy broads I have been tellin' you about, a blonde to be specific, perched on a bar stool and starin' right at me. I know this to be true, 'cause though for a minute I thought she was lookin' at someone else, as soon as our eyes meet, she closes one eye in a broad wink and smiles.

"Nunzio," I sez, duckin' my head and turnin' my back on her. "There is one more problem I have neglected to mention to you."

"What's that?"

"Well, though my manners with broads are perhaps not as polished as they should be, they are nonetheless the best I have managed to acquire over the years. That is to say, I am normally on my best behavior with females, so the idea of tryin' to act so offensive that they call for help is not particularly comfortable to me. Mind you, I am sayin' I would have difficulty doin' this with the ordinary broads I am accustomed to dealin' with, and to tell you the truth, I find the kind of classy broads that hang out here more than a little intimidatin'. I'm not sure I can start a conversation with one, much less summon the courage to try to be offensive."

"Well, I don't think that starting a conversation is going to be a problem," Nunzio sez.

"Why not?"

"Because the lady in question is on her way over to our table already."

Surprised, I swing my head back around to check things out for myself... and come dangerously close to plantin' my nose in the broad's cleavage, as she is much closer to our table than Nunzio had indicated.

"Oops... Sorry!" I sez, though it occurred to me as I said it that it was not a great start to bein' offensive.

"No problem," she sez. "A girl likes to feel appreciated. Mind if I join you?"

Somethin' about the way she grins while sayin' this is familiar... or at least, decidedly un-ladylike. Before I can comment, however, Nunzio has taken over.

"Certainly. In fact, you can have my chair... I was just leaving anyway. Catch you later, Guido... and remember what we were talking about."

With that, he gives me a big wink and wanders off, leavin' me alone with the skirt... who wastes no time plantin' her curvaceous bottom on the chair my cousin has so graciously vacated.

"So... I haven't seen you in here before."

"What?"

I have been so busy thinkin' about what I am goin' to do to Nunzio to repay him for his 'graciousness' that I nearly miss the broad's openin' gambit.

"Oh. No, we just got into town this week. This seems to be turnin' out to be our main hangout, though."

"Hey, that's terrific! This is one of my favorite spots. It's my first time in this week, though. Girl's got to do the rounds to keep up with what's going on in town... like when new soldiers arrive."

Although I have been feelin' self conscious about meetin' one of these high class skirts, this one seems real easy to talk to... like I'd known her for years. What's more, she is certainly not at all hard on the eyes, if you know what I mean.

"Say," I sez, "can I get you somthin' to drink? A wine spritzer, maybe?"

"Bourbon. Rocks. Water back."

"Say what?"

I mean, it isn't just that she drinks stronger hootch than I would have expected, it is the way she rattled it off. I decide it is not this chick's first time into a bar... a decision made easier by the fact she has already told me as much.

"Better still," she sez, "isn't there somewhere else we can go?"

This is a rough one, Abdul's is the only joint in town I have frequented so far.

"Ummmm..." I sez, thinkin' fast, "I have heard of some place around here where there's open stage entertainment."

Mind you, I am not wild about takin' this skirt somewhere where I might run into my commandin' officer, but I figure she'll be impressed with my willingness to spring for a good time.

"I was thinking someplace more like the rooms upstairs," she sez, leanin' forward to smile at me real close.

I am taken a little aback by the forwardness of this suggestion, though I suppose I

114

shouldn't be surprised. When a high- class babe like this approaches a low-brow Joe like me in a bar, she is not usually after witty conversation... which, in my case, is fortunate.

(AUTHOR'S NOTE: It has been brought to my attention by some of my test readers that the concepts in this chapter and those that immediately follow are a marked change of pace from the normal MYTH content. In this, I fear it may be my sad duty to introduce to some readers for the first time the horrifying reality that there *are* a few sick, twisted, perverted individuals who approach members of the opposite sex in singles bars for purposes other than pleasant conversation! I feel free to identify them as such in this book, since it is a well known fact that such blots on the shining history of mankind *do not read*, making me relatively safe from legal action. Incidentally, this is also why the question "Read any good books lately?" has become such a popular way of screening whom one does or doesn't talk to under such circumstances. I will leave it to you how to answer if the question is ever addressed to you. Meanwhile, back to the story...)

As I was sayin' before I was so *rudely interrupted*, I am at a bit of a loss as to how to respond to this advance.

"Right now?" I sez. "Don't you want to talk for a while first?"

"What's wrong? Don't you like me?" she sez, startin' to pout a little. "Should I go peddle my wares somewhere else?"

"Peddle?"

"Watch it," she sez, flat and nasty. "It's a figure of speech."

"Oh."

I am vastly relieved to hear this. The only thing more depressin' to a sensitive guy like me than learnin' that a female is interested in him for his body and not his mind is learnin' that her *real* interest is in his wallet.

"Well?" she sez, cockin' an eyebrow at me.

Though I am, perhaps, a little dense at pickin' up cues from a skirt, let it never be said I am slow once the message has gotten through. Scant seconds later I have acquired the key to a room from Frumple and am leadin' this vision of loveliness up the narrow stairs... well, followin' her, actually, as experience has taught me that this gives one an excellent view of the sway of her hips, which is to me still one of the most beautiful and hypnotic sights in any dimension.

In a masterful display of control, I manages not to fumble with the key whilst unlockin' the door, and even stand aside to let her enter first.

Bein' a broad, she whips out one of those foldin' mirrors and starts checkin' her makeup even before I finish lockin' the door behind us.

"So," I sez, over my shoulder, "What do you want to do first?"

To be honest with youse, at this point I have no interest at all in creatin' a hassle. Instead, I am thankin' my lucky stars that a skirt like this would give a lug like me a second look, and hopin' we can get on with things before she changes her mind.

"Well," she sez, "You could start by bringing me up to date on how you and Nunzio have been doing."

It takes a moment for this to sink in, but when it does, I knows just what to say.

116

"Say what?" I sez, spinnin' around.

The skirt what I come upstairs with is nowhere to be seen. Instead, I've got a different broad in the room with me. One with green hair and...

"Hi, Guido!" she sez. "Great disguise, huh?"

Chapter 10

"Now, here's my plan!"
R. Burns

TANANDA? Is that you?"

My surprise is not entirely due to my not havin' spotted who it is what has been cadgin' drinks from me all evening... though I hadn't. Rather I am more than a little startled by her appearance, which has changed considerably since we parted company at the beginnin' of this mission.

Tananda is normally a spectacular lookin-skirt with an impressive mane of green hair. While she has never chosen to present the formal, every-hair-in-place-self-presentation favored by most of the broads what hang out at the sushi bar, optin' instead for a casual wind-blown look, I am sufficiently versed in the secrets of the female gender to be aware that the latter look is as, or more, difficult to establish and maintain as the former, and often harder to carry off. All of which is to say Tananda is usually very attentive to and careful of her looks.

What I am currently seein', however, is someone who looks like she has been on the wrong end of a bad accident. Most of the hair is missin' from one side of her head, along with the correspondin' eyebrow, and the other side of her face is marred by a big bruise which seems to be fadin', but still looks painful. Havin' both given and received more than my share of the latter type of injury, I can estimate with fair accuracy the force of the blow necessary to produce such spectacular results... and it must have been a doozey.

"Sorry for the horror show," she sez, puttin' away her disguise mirror after takin' one last peek, as if to see whether things have changed since the last time she looked, "but it's been a rough assignment so far."

"What... What happened to you?" I sez, findin' my voice at last. "Who did this to you?"

I mean, we had all known there might be some trouble associated with this mission, but nobody likes to see a beautiful skirt get worked over.

"Would you believe it was our own team?" she sez, flashin' a quick smile, though I knew it hurt.

"Come again?"

"The hair is courtesy of Gleep," she explained. "I guess it was an accident. I must have gotten between him and dinner or something. Anyway, it's not as bad as it looks... or could have been. Chumley saw it coming even

119

if I didn't and got me out of the way of the worst of it... which is both where the bruise came from and why I'm not complaining about it. Honestly, you should see what happened to the wall that was behind me at the time."

"Speakin' of which, where are Chumley and Gleep?"

For the first time in our conversation, Tananda starts lookin' uncomfortable.

"They've... ah... headed back to Big Julie's. Actually, big brother's in a bit worse shape than I am, so rather than have him trying to work with his arm in a sling, I told him to take Gleep somewhere out of the action and stay with him for awhile. It's funny, you know? I still can't figure what set Gleep off... but until we can get a handle on it, I figure he's more of a danger than a help on this assignment. Anyway, I decided to stay on and use this disguise gizmo to see if I could do anything to help the cause on my own. I sure couldn't do much worse than we were doing as a team."

Somethin' was tuggin' at the back of my mind... somethin' that Nunzio had said about his last assignment and bein' nervous about workin' with Gleep again. I couldn't put my finger on it, though, and seein' as how the discussion was makin' Tananda uncomfortable, I decided not to pursue the subject. I did, however, make a mental note to talk with Nunzio about it when we had a chance.

"Sounds like things weren't goin' too well even before the accident," I sez, pickin' up on her last aside.

"You can say that again," Tananda sez, heavin' a little sigh. "We were trying to work a variation on the old badger game... you know, where I give a soldier the come on, then Chumley bursts in and raises a ruckus because the guy's compromising his sister's honor?"

"I know the scam," I sez, 'cause I do... though I've never run it or been victimized by it myself. Still, it's a time-tested, classic gambit.

"Well, it wasn't working anywhere near as well as we would have hoped. Most of the soldiers around here are under orders to keep their hands off the local women, and if I upped the voltage to make them forget their orders, then the locals would spot what I was doing and take the position that I was asking for whatever attentions I got."

"Gee, that's tough," I said. "It musta been hard on you... particularly if you was workin' injured."

I still didn't like the way that bruise was healin', and it must have shown in my voice 'cause Tananda leans forward and puts a hand on my arm.

"I'm all right, Guido, really... though it's sweet of you to be worried. I've gotten a lot worse just rough-housing with Chumley... honest."

Realizin' that her big brother is a troll, I can well believe that Tananda is used to gettin' dinged up a bit in family squabbles. Right now, however, there is somethin' else weighin' on my mind.

You see, Tananda's touch was real soft and warm when she laid her hand on my arm, and it gets me to thinkin' again about the original reason I had for bringin' her up to this room. As I said before, it has been a long time since I have been alone with a skirt on anythin' resemblin' an intimate basis... But Tananda is *still* a business associate, and as with any profession, it is unwise at best to allow oneself to become intimately involved with a fellow worker. Besides, she has never indicated to me any interest beyond friendship... or maybe a big sister. Still, it was real nice to have woman touchin' me...

"Umm... All right. If you say so," I sez, movin' slightly to break the physical contact between us. "We was just assigned here ourselves, so we haven't had a chance to do much of anythin'. I think maybe we should try to figure out how Nunzio and me can work the same area as you without us gettin' in each others' way."

"Don't be silly, Guido. Since you're here, we can all work together!"

"Come again?"

"Think about it," she sez, gettin' all bouncy in her eagerness. "I've been having trouble finding soldiers to take the bait on my little routine, but *you're soldiers*, so it can make both our jobs easier. If we're working *both* sides of the game, we can control exactly how we want things to go."

I make a sincere effort to ignore her bouncin' whilst I try to think of a good reason not to go along with her suggestion. Somehow I am not sure my actin' skills are up to *pretendin'* to be physically forward with Tananda... but I am even less enthusiastic about havin' Nunzio take the part.

"I dunno, Tananda," I sez, reluctant like. "I'm not so sure that's a good idea. I mean, we might pull it off once... but if we're successful in our play-actin', then Nunzio and me end up in the stockade and out of action for the duration."

"Oh yeah?" she sez, cockin' her remainin' eyebrow at me. "So what were you thinking would happen when you brought me up here this evening?"

"Ummm..." I sez, recallin' that, unfortuitously, takin' the Fifth Amendment only works in court.

"Never mind, Guido," she grins. "I withdraw the question. Tell you what, though. If being directly involved makes you uneasy, just line me up with one of your army buddies. You've been in long enough that you should have a pretty good idea of who we can sucker."

I find that I am not wild about this idea either; first, because it seems like a dirty trick to play on any of the crew what's been workin' with Nunzio and me the last few weeks, and second, because I find I am not overjoyed with the idea of *anybody* pawin' Tananda. Still, I had to accept that we was gonna have to break *somebody's* eggs to get this omelette made, and that Tananda is right, it would be easier and quicker to do if we set the thing up ourselves.

"Okay, Tananda," I sez. "We'll try it that way."

"Are you okay, Guido?" she sez, peerin' at me concerned like. "You sound a little flat."

"I'm all right. I'll tell youse though Tananda, this assignment is gettin' me down a little."

"Well cheer up, things may have been rocky so far, but working together, we should be able to make some progress. Tell you what, find Nunzio and fill him in what we're doing. Then we'll meet back here and give it a try... say, tomorrow night?"

"Sure, why not?"

"In the meantime," she sez, opening' her disguise mirror again and startin' to fiddle with the knobs, "come on downstairs and *I'll* buy *you* a drink or two."

For a minute that sounds like a good idea. Then I remember Frumple.

"I think we'd better cool it, Tananda. We gotta be careful about how much we're seen together here."

"What do you mean?"

"The reason we're hangin' out here is we found out that the proprietor's a Deveel. The trouble is, he seems to know the Boss and has some kind of grudge against him. So far, he doesn't know we're connected with the Boss, but if he gets suspicious..."

"A Deveel?"

"Yeah. Says his name is Frumple."

"Frumple? So he's back in operation again, is he?"

"You know him?"

"Sure. He teamed up with Isstvan against us back when I first met Skeeve... and you're right, if he gets suspicious, a disguise spell wouldn't keep him from figuring out who I am."

"Maybe we should wait and try to run our gambit somewhere other than here," I sez, tryin' to keep the hope out of my voice.

"No need," Tananda grins. "As long as he doesn't make the connection between us beforehand, we should still be able to pull it off tomorrow night. In fact, it'll be killing two birds with one stone, in a manner of speaking. I don't mind doing Frumple a bit of dirt in the course of action, and it looks like his place will be at

124

ground zero when the fireworks start. By the time he puts it together, we'll be long gone."

"Swell," I sez, with more enthusiasm than I am feelin'. "Then we're all set. Youse go ahead and leave first. I'll stay up here awhile and give youse a head start."

As soon as she is gone, I settle myself to try to sort out my misgivin's about how things are goin' on this assignment. It doesn't take long to figure out that I am sufferin' under a burden of conflictin' loyalties.

Youse may find this surprisin' from someone in my line of work, but loyalty and betrayin' trust counts very high up in my books... which is one of the things I have always admired about the M.Y.T.H. Inc. crew as they all seem to value the same thing.

In the past, I've managed to balance my loyalties between the Boss and the Mob, as the strange approach the Boss takes to things has not directly threatened any of the Mob's interests. This current situational, however, is turnin' out to be a horse of a different caliber.

In plannin' to stir up trouble between the civilians and the army, I am violatin' the trust placed in me as a representative of the army... but I have managed to rationalize this as it is my *reason* for joinin' the army in the first place, so in this matter I am actin' kinda like a spy with my loyalty clearly with the Boss.

Nunzio has convinced me that I am not violatin' my deal with Frumple by usin' his place as a site for our mischief, as it falls outside the agreement we made. This strikes me as a little shaky, but I can be flexible when the occasion calls for it.

This latest plan, though, of settin' up

someone in your squad to be the fall guy is *real* hard to see as anythin' except betrayin' a friend. Still, Tananda is right... it *is* the best way to be sure that things go the way we want 'em to.

Thinkin' it over real heard, I finally come up with an answer: What I gotta do is think of it as a joke on a buddy. Okay, maybe it's a dubious joke... like poppin' a paper bag behind someone who's gettin' ready to blow a safe... but as long as the notable in question does not end up permanently damaged or incarcerated as a result, it can be passed off as a joke.

Now, my only concern is tryin' to make sure that whoever we pick has a sense of humor... a real *good* sense of humor!

Chapter 11

"That's why the lady is a tramp!"
B. Midler

Hoooo-ey! The place is sure jumpin' tonight!" Shu Flie exclaims, leanin' back in his chair to survey the room.

"You kin say that again, Shu," his brother sez. "Hey! Lookit that one over there!"

Any way youse look at it, the Flie brothers run a class act... though politeness will forbid my commentin' on *which* class. For a change, however, I am inclined to agree with them.

This is our first weekend in Twixt, much less here at Abdul's, and the bar is packed to overflowin'. In fact, if we hadn't been drinkin' here since early afternoon, it's doubtful we would have a table at all. As it is, we are entrenched at our regular table with a good view of the bar... or, to be more specific the de-rears arrayed along the bar... as well as the de-fronts when they turn around. Believe me, speakin' as a well-traveled demon, youse don't get scenery like this just anywhere!

Unfortunately, my enjoyment of the view is marred by my distraction over the comin' events.

"Whatdaya think Swatter?" Shu sez, turnin' his attention to me. "You ever see women like this before?"

"Oh, they're not bad," I sez, cranin' my neck to scan the crowd.

It has occurred to me that Tananda will probably be in disguise when she arrives, and it will therefore be difficult for me to recognize her unless she gives me some kind of signal.

"Not bad? Listen to this, guys! All this beautiful woman- flesh, and all Swatter can say is 'They're not bad'!"

"Really, Swatter," Junebug sez. "You just don't see beautiful women like this in the army!"

This earns him a dangerous scowl from Spyder, but he misses it completely as he is feelin' his drinks more than a little at this point.

"Nice crowd for a fight. Know what I mean, cuz?" Nunzio murmurs in my ear low enough so no one else can hear.

"I dunno," I sez, scannin' the crowd again. "I don't see a single one of these white collar types that even Bee couldn't take without half tryin'."

"That's what I mean," Nunzio grins, and helps himself to another swallow from his drink.

As you can maybe tell from his behavior, the hesitations I have been experiencin' about settin' up one of our buddies has not bothered my cousin in the least. If anything, he seems to be lookin' forward to a bit of trouble.

"Watch my chair," I sez, standing up. "I'm goin' to the bar for a refill."

Like I said, the place is mobbed, and in typical tightfisted Deveel type fashion, Frumple has not incurred the added overhead of puttin' on extra help, so if youse wants to get a drink sometime *before* the next Ice Age, it is necessitated that youse belly up to the bar to get your refill directly from the bartender. If youse is wonderin' why someone as greedy as Frumple is willin' to miss the extra income generated by a higher turnover of drinks, let me restore your faith by explainin' that he makes it up both by waterin' the hootch *and* by increasin' his unit revenue... which is to say he raises his prices as the crowds get bigger.

Strangely enough, neither the weaker drinks nor the sky-high prices seem to faze this crowd in the least. I figure this is because they feel that payin' three times the normal goin' fare for a drink will screen out the rabble one usually has to tolerate when drinkin' in a public place, thereby insurin' that they are makin' their passes at folks of an equal or higher income bracket, and as to the watered drinks... well, the only reason I can come up with that they aren't complainin' about this is that they probably figure that booze is unhealthy, so a weak drink is somehow healthier than a strong one.

You see, I have ascertained through eavesdroppin' that health, and specifically healthy consumables, is a *very* big issue with these upwardly mobile folks. It's like they're used to thinkin' that you can get anythin' with enough money... and they've gotten it into their heads that by spendin' more for health foods and health drinks, they is never gonna die. Of course, they spend so much time worryin' and naggin' each other about good health, that they tend to generate sufficient stress to keel over and croak from heart attacks... but this seems to be an acceptable, if not desirable, option as it is generally viewed as "the high pressure which is the mark of a successful career person" and therefore has become somethin' of a badge of status. What is somehow overlooked in all this is that much of the stress is needless anxiety they inflict upon themselves by worryin' about such things as status and health foods.

Perhaps it is because of the high-risk nature of my chosen profession, but I personally have no illusions of my own immortality. The way I see it, there are enough unpredictable things in life that can kill you that the only rational approach to life is to take what little pleasures youse can as they presents themselves, so that when your number comes up, you can at least die knowin' you've had a full and happy life. I think that life should be more than an exercise in self-denial, and even if I was guaranteed that I could live forever by abstainin', I'd probably continue my occasional indulgences. I mean, who wants to live forever... particularly if that life has been designed to be borin' and devoid of pleasure?

I am reflectin' on this when a broad elbows her way in next to me at the bar. At first I think she is just really desperate for a drink, which as I said is understandable considerin' the slow service, and step aside, usin' my not inconsiderable bulk to make room for her.

"Got my target picked out for me?"

It takes a second for me to realize that I am the one this question is bein' addressed to, as she sez it casual without lookin' at me direct.

"Tananda?" I sez, lookin' at her hard.

She is wearin' a different disguise tonight... a shoulder length cloud of dark curls and a dress made of some clingy fabric that... well, shows off everything she's got underneath it.

"Don't look at me!" she hisses, quietly grindin' a heel onto my toe to emphasize her point while glancin' at the ceilin'. "We aren't supposed to know each other... remember?"

"Oh, right... sorry."

I go back to starin' into my glass, doin' my best to ignore her presence... which is not easy as the crowd is pressin' a considerable amount of her against me as we're standin' there.

"Okay, who's our pigeon?"

"You see the two broad shouldered guys at our table? The loud ones? I figure the one on the left will do you just fine."

Guido and I have decided on Shu Flie for our victim. Of the crew, we're probably the least fond of the Flie brothers, and while either of them would probably serve our purposes, Shu is the more dominant and might start trouble if Tananda made a play for his brother instead of him. As our objective is to cause trouble between the army and the civilians, fightin' within our own ranks would be counter-productive.

"Who's the yummy one across the table from the animals?"

131

I sneak a peek behind me to be sure who she's talkin' about."

"That? That's Junebug. He used to be an actor or a dancer or somethin'."

"He'll do," she sez firmly, a predatory note creepin' into her voice.

I refrain from lookin', but have a strong suspicion she is lickin' her lips... mentally, if not physically.

"I don't think that's such a hot idea, Tananda," I sez. "There's sort of a thing goin' between him and Spyder. At least, she's got a thing for him."

"Who?"

"Spyder. The chick in uniform sittin' next to him."

"*That's* female?"

While, as you know, I had much the same reaction the first time I met Spyder, for some reason it bothers me hearin' it from Tananda.

"Don't let the hair fool you," I sez, "She's pretty tough."

"That's sweet of you, Guido," Tananda sez, misunderstandin' what I was sayin', "but the day I can't hold my own against *that*, I'll hang it up. Well, off to work."

"What I mean is..." I try to say, but Tananda is already gone, slitherin' after Junebug like some kind of feline snake sidlin' up to a drunk canary.

This is just swell! While I suppose our "army vs. civilians" objective could be achieved by a cat fight between Tananda and Spyder, it wasn't exactly what we had in mind when we planned this scenario.

As it turns out, though, I needn't have worried. Watchin' from the bar, I see Junebug re-

spond to Tananda's come-on like a first of-
fender latchin' onto his lawyer, and instead of
startin' a fight, Spyder just stands up and
stomps out of the place with a scowl on her
face and her ears laid back in her multicolored
hair.

"Who's that talking to your buddy?"
Frumple sez, materializin' in front of me.

I make a big show of lookin' back at our
table.

"Just a broad," I shrug casual like, sig-
nallin' for a refill. "Why?"

"No reason. For a minute there I thought
she looked familiar is all."

He heads off down the bar to fetch my
drink, leavin' me a little uneasy. I tell myself
there is no reason why the Deveel should recognize Tananda, as her current disguise bears
no resemblance to her regular appearance.
Still, he is an unstable element in the current
equation, and I would just as soon keep him
out of it entirely, if possible.

"I thought we were targeting Shu Flie,"
Nunzio sez, easin' in beside me at the bar. It
may have been crowded where we were, but
people usually manage to make room for someone Nunzio's size, especially if he's talkin' to
someone my size.

"We were," I sez. "But Tananda has her
own ideas on the subject."

"Well it sure put Spyder's nose out of joint.
I don't think I've ever seen her so mad. Unless
it was the time..."

"Hey... Abdul!"

It was Junebug, standin' right behind us
tryin' to get Frumple's attention. He has his
arm draped around Tananda's shoulders, but if

you look real close youse can see that she is actually holdin' up most of his weight.

"Yeah? What do you want?"

Though he wasn't particularly pleasant about it, the speed with which any of our crew could get the Deveel's attention was evidence that he hadn't forgotten we all knew his secret.

"I... we need... a room."

"There aren't any available."

Frumple starts to turn away, only to find his movement is restricted... specifically by my cousin who has reached across the bar and taken hold of his shoulder.

"Give him a room," Nunzio sez, soft-like.

Now, when Nunzio talks quiet like that, it usually means he is about to lose his temper... which, in this case, is understandable. I mean, we have put an awful lot of trouble into this setup to have it thwarted by anything silly like room availability.

"But there aren't any..."

"Give him the room you keep for yourself. You're going to be too busy down here to use it for awhile."

"I'm not *that* busy," the Deveel argues, tryin' to twist out of Nunzio's grip. "And if..."

"You *could* be a lot busier... if you know what I mean," Nunzio sez, startin' to tighten his hand.

"All right! Okay! Here!" Frumple sez, producin' a key from his pocket and passin' it to Junebug. "Last door on the right!"

"Thanks, Nunzio," Junebug calls over his shoulder as he and Tananda weave their way toward the stairs.

My cousin waits until they are out of sight before he bothers to release his grip on

Frumple.

"Now, see how nice it makes you feel to bring a little happiness into someone else's life?"

The Deveel bares his teeth in a silent snarl, then heads off down the bar to tend to the growin' number of shouters.

"Well, *that* didn't take long," I sez, lookin' at the stairs where Tananda and Junebug have vanished.

"Not surprising, really," Nunzio sez with a leer. "I mean, how long would *you* dawdle around if Tananda invited you into her room?"

If you surmise from this that I have not given my cousin a *complete* account of my meetin' with Tananda, you are correct. I decide to change the subject.

"One question, cousin," I sez, takin' a sip of my drink. "How are we supposed to know when to intrude on the proceedin's?"

"I dunno, I guess we wait until we hear Tananda start callin' for help."

I swivel my head around and stare at him.

"Nunzio," I sez, "has it occurred to you that with the racket goin' on down here, she can shoot off a cannon and we won't be able to hear her?"

This brings a scowl to his face.

"Good point," he sez, borrowin' a sip from my drink.

"Good point? Is that all you got to say?" I am startin' to get worked up now. "What do you think is gonna happen if we miss our cue and *don't* break things up?"

"Hmmm... well, if we don't rescue her, then Tananda's gonna have to deal with Junebug herself."

"...Which means one of our squad ends up in the hospital," I finishes for him. "Either that or *Tananda* takes a bunch of lumps waitin' for us to show up like we said we would."

"Like I said... good point."

"Well, *I'm* not gonna just sit here," I sez, standin' up. "You comin' with me?"

"You mean bust in on 'em right now?"

"That's *just* what I mean. Why not? They've already been up there for awhile."

At this point, I am besieged by mental images of Tananda bein' pawed by Junebug... all the while callin' vainly for us to help her.

"Just a second, Guido," Nunzio sez, then raises his voice. "Hey! Bee!"

Our junior magician comes scuttlin' over to us.

"What is it, Nunzio?"

"I want you to go out and find some police and bring them back here."

"Police? But why..."

"Just do it! Okay?"

"Sure Nunzio. City police or Military Police?"

"Both, if you can manage it. Now get going."

He turns to me as Bee goes sprintin' out into the night.

"All right, Guido. It's party time!"

Chapter 12

"It sure looks to me like a big night tonight!"
Arthur, rex

In our plannin', we had neglected to establish a means by which Tananda
was to let us know which room they was gonna
be in. (Oversights such as this is why I am
usually willin' to let someone else... like the
Boss... do our plannin' for us!) Fortuitously, the
Deveel had given them directions loud enough
for us to hear at the same time as he was
handin' them the key, so we have no trouble
findin' where we are supposed to be.

"I don't hear anything... do you?" Nunzio
sez, cockin' his head outside the door.

By now, however, I am gettin' a head of
steam up and am in no mood to quibble over
details.

"Maybe you should have thought of that

before you sent Bee for the cops," I sez, backin'
up to get a runnin' start. "But since you did, we
are kinda committed to be there when the waltz
starts... know what I mean?"

"Well, just remember that the key to this
working is to try to promote confusion when-
ever possible."

"That shouldn't be hard," I snarl, and
launch myself at the door.

I have specifically mentioned our objective
of "confusion" so that youse folks readin' this
will not think your brains have suddenly gone
Fruit Loops while tryin' to sort out this next
series of events... that is, it's *supposed* to be
confusion'!

Anyway, the door goes down, as doors are
inclined to do when I hit them goin' full tilt,
and the two of us pile into the room... which I
am not too busy to notice is considerably nicer
than the room Frumple gave me yesterday.

To our startlement, there is no altercation
occurrin' in the room... at least, not until we
arrive. Tananda and Junebug are in a huddle
on the sofa, but any noise she is makin' is not
screams of outrage. Still, as we have made our
entrance, my cousin and me have little choice
but to continue with the script as originally
planned.

Nunzio latches on to Junebug, liftin' him
clear of the sofa whilst I turns my attentions to
Tananda.

"Are you okay, lady??" I sez in my loudest
voice, which projects pretty well thanks to my
old drama coach. *"Just take it easy!!"*

"Damn it, Guido! Not yet!!" she hisses,
glarin' at me as she struggles into a sittin' position.

138

DEVEEL BRAND SNAKE MASSAGE OIL

139

Now, this is not part of our planned dialogue, and I glance over at Junebug quick like to see if he has noticed that Tananda has let it slip that we know each other. I need not have concerned myself.

Nunzio is holdin' Junebug high enough that his feet are not touchin' the floor, hangin' onto him by the front of his uniform while shakin' him hard. Of course, on the out-stroke, he is also slammin' our colleague into the wall in a repeated manner solidly enough to shake the buildin'. He has done this to me on a couple of occasions, so I can state from personal experience that while it may *look* like he is tryin' to help you clear your head, the actualities of the situational is that after hittin' the wall a few times, you're lucky to remember your name, much less why he is carryin' on in this manner.

"Calm down, Junebug!" my cousin is shoutin'. *"She isn't worth it!! We don't want no trouble!!!"*

Seein' as how Junebug is distracted, which I can tell by the way his eyes are rollin' around independent-like in his head, I turn my attention to Tananda once more.

"Look, Tananda," I growl, lowerin' my voice so's only she can hear me, "I apologize if our timin' is less than exact. You can beat on me for it later. In the meantime, might I point out that the curtain is already up and you have been entrusted with a rather important role in our performance?"

"But we were just starting to..." she pauses here and draws a long, ragged breath. "Oh... All right!"

With this, she reaches up, takes hold of the

shoulder of her dress, and rips it diagonally across her body down to the hip... in doin' so givin' me a quick glimpse of a lot more of Tananda than it has previously been my privilege to view.

"He was going to... Oh, it was just awful! What kind of people are you, anyway?"

She pauses in her hysterics.

"Guido!" she sez, urgent like.

I am still starin' at the portion of the dress she is now tryin' to hold together with one hand.

"Hmmm? Oh... Yeah! *Just take it easy, lady!!"* I sez, avertin' my eyes as I am a little embarrassed. *"He didn't mean nothin'!!"*

"Get him away from me!!! Just get him away!!!"

That cue I can remember.

"Come on Nunzio," I sez. "Let's get him out of here!"

With that, we each grab Junebug by one arm and usher him out of the room through the crowd that's startin' to gather. I look back at Tananda and give her a wink, but she just sticks her tongue out at me quick-like before continuin' her hysterics.

"WHAT KIND OF A PLACE IS THIS?" she screams after us. *"Letting animals like that mix with decent people..."*

I lose the rest of her performance as we are carryin' Junebug down to the main floor by now.

The crowd what has been outside the room was nothin' compared to what was waitin' for us in the bar. Everybody in the place is crowdin' around to see what is goin' on... well, crowdin' at a distance like folks do when they don't want to be right up close to the action. Toward the back, I can see the uniforms of some of the local constabulary, though they are havin' trouble reachin' us through the heavy traffic. Of the Military Police there is no sign... so I figure we will just have to start without them.

"What's going on up there?" Frumple demands, appearin' at my side.

"Here," I sez out of the side of my mouth, pushin' some money into his hand. "Take this."

"What's this for?" he sez, scowlin' at my offerin'.

"That should cover the bar bill for our table since this afternoon."

"Your bar bill?" he frowns. "I don't get it. We had a deal. I give you free drinks, and you don't bust up my place or tell anyone... my secret."

"Don't worry," I sez, showin' him a few teeth. "Your secret is safe."

"Then what... Hey! Wait a minute! You aren't going to..."

Just then, the police reach us.

Now, earlier Nunzio and me was commentin' how there wasn't anyone in the bar who could give us a run for our money. This situational changes when these cops roll in. There are four of them, and while none of them looks particularly tough physically bein' uniformly soft around the middle, there is a steadiness in their eyes that anyone in the business can spot as the mark of someone what don't get particularly rattled when trouble starts.

"All right!" the biggest one of 'em says, steppin' up to us. "What's going on here?"

As you might guess, people of Nunzio's and my profession are not overly fond of the authorities of the law, particularly the street variety, and we usually give them wide berth. So in actual confrontation such as this, it is not too difficult for us to act unpleasant.

"What kind of town is this?" Nunzio bellows, *glarin' around at the crowd. "A man in uniform tries to have a quiet drink... and the next thing you know, some bimbo is trying to set him up for a bum rap!!"*

"Just take it easy soldier," the cop sez, friendly-like. "You're among friends now. There are a couple of us who were in the service ourselves once."

This is somethin' we hadn't counted on. The last thing we need right now is for the cops to act reasonable. I figure it is about time I take a hand in the proceedin's personally.

"Oh yeah?" I sneers. *"What happened? You chicken out when it looked like there might actually be some fightin' to be done? Figured it was safer hasslin' drunks than gettin' shot at?"*

"Cool down, soldier," the cop smiles, but I can see his lips are real tight. "Let's just step outside and discuss this."

"You hear that?" Nunzio shouts to the Flie brothers who are still holdin' down our table. *"They don't mind taking our money for drinks... but when we catch 'em tryin' to roll one of our boys, THEN they try to send us packing!"*

"Oh yeah?" Shu Flie bristles and stands up, crowdin' toward us followed close by his brother. "Well if they want us out of here, they're gonna have to *throw* us out!"

Caught between us on one side and the Flie brothers on the other, the cops start gettin' nervous, swivelin' their heads back and forth tryin' to keep an eye on all of us.

"Now hold on a minute!" the cop we was talkin' to sez. "Who are you saying was trying to roll you?"

"That floozie upstairs!" Nunzio snarls, jerkin' a thumb back over his shoulder. *"She gave our buddy the big come on... crawlin' all over him, you know? Then when we go up to see if he's all right 'cause he's been drinkin', she's goin' through his pockets!"*

"That's right!" Hy Flie sez. "We were sittin' right over there when this bombshell starts playing up to Junebug here!"

"Of course, they stick up for each other!" one of the guys in the front of the crowd snorts to the fellow next to him.

I don't think he meant to be heard, but Shu Flie was standin' right beside him and caught it.

"Are you callin' my brother a liar?" he sez, startin' for the loudmouth.

I'm thinking we got the fight in the bag, but one of the cops gets between 'em holdin' them apart with a hand on each of their chests.

"Back off! *Both of you!*" he orders. "We're going to get to the bottom of this..."

"GET YOUR HANDS OFF THAT SOL-DIER!!"

The Military Police have arrived and come pushin' through the crowd to join our discussion group.

*"Military personnel are to be handled by the MPs and **not** pushed around by some cop with a chip on his shoulder!"*

The sergeant in charge of the MPs is a real bruiser and just the kind of Joe I wanted to see... not too bright and dog-stubborn. He has three of his buddies with him, so we *really* outnumber the cops. Then I see some more police uniforms comin' through the door and have to revise my count again. It looks like a real party shapin' up.

"We *weren't* pushing him around!" the first cop sez, steppin' in nose to nose with the MP sergeant. "What's more, this investigation involves a civilian, so until we find out what happened..."

"We caught some bimbo tryin' to roll one of our boys!" Shu Flie shouts at the MP. *"And now they're all tryin' to cover up for her!"*

"Is that so!" the MP scowls, glarin' around at the bar. "These soldiers risk their lives to keep things safe for you, and *this* is the thanks they get?"

What a great guy, I think. What a great, gullible, thick-headed guy. He could probably get this fight started all by himself... if we let him.

"I resent that remark!" our cop snarls, finally startin' to lose it. *"We risk our lives too, you know!"*

"Oh excuse me! I forgot!" the MP smiles nasty like "You're in constant danger of choking to death on a doughnut!"

"Doughnut, is it?" the cop sez, lookin' around slow at the other cops... maybe to count heads and check the odds before decidin' what to do or say next.

I turn my head to sneak a wink at Nunzio, just in time to see Tananda make her entrance from the stairs.

"THERE THEY ARE!!!" she shrieks. *"Those are the soldiers that attacked me!!"*

It would seem that she has been busy with her disguise gizmo, because the bruise I have earlier commented on is now clearly in evidence... although to an experienced eye such as my own, it is obvious that it is not a recent injury. Of course, bein' Tananda and havin' a flair for the dramatic, she has not stopped there. While the dress she is wearin' is the same color as the one she had on earlier, its hemline and fit are a lot more modest that the hot outfit she used to get Junebug's attention... a *lot* more. On top of that, her wild, sexy hairdo now looks more like some librarian's maidenly bun what has been pawed to pieces. The *real* beauty of all this, however, is that she is standin' where the cops can see her, but the MPs can't! Of course, the crowd can see her, too.

"*That's* no floozie!" the guy what mouthed off earlier sez.

"Hey! I think she works with me!" someone else chimes in.

"See what happens when they let *soldiers* in here?"

The crowd is startin' to get ugly, but to give the cop credit, he tries to calm things down.

"**Just relax, everybody!**" he hollers. "**We're** handling this!"

Then he turns back to the MP, his face all grim like.

"We've got to get to the bottom of this, ser-geant," he sez. "I want you to hold *those* three men..."

As he's sayin' this, he raises his hand to point in our direction.

Now there is a gag that Nunzio and I have pulled so often that we don't even have to look at each other now to know what to do. We are still holdin' Junebug up by his arms, and the cop is close enough that when he tries to point at us, it's an easy matter for us to move Junebug sideways in front of his hand... then let go!

Unless you are watchin' real close at the right moment, this looks exactly like the cop took a poke at Junebug and decked him!

Realizin' the already tense nature of the situational, this is a little like beatin' on a blastin' cap with a hammer.

The MP starts to reach for the cop, but I get there first... mostly 'cause I know what is comin' and have a head start.

"Let me!" I sez, then I do somethin' I've been wantin' to do all my life.

I lay my best punch on a cop... in front of witnesses!

Chapter 13

"Weren't you expecting me?"
J. Rambo

Me and Nunzio have a bit of a wait before the company commander shows up at his office. This is fine by me, as it gives me a chance to stop my nose from bleedin' quite so much, and we even talk the MPs guardin' us into gettin' some disinfectant to put on our knuckles.

If from this youse infers that it was quite a brawl, youse is correct. It was... and what's more we are the clear winners. Now, the civilian cops may have different opinions regardin' this, but we was still standin' at the end of it and they wasn't so I feel we are justified in claimin' the victory.

As I mentioned, our guards are okay guys

and in a pretty good mood to boot, which is understandable as they was fightin' on our side in the fracas under discussion. We have a pretty good time with them while we are waitin', swappin' tales from the fight that were at least partially true, interruptin' each other all the time with comments of "Did you see it when I...?" and "Yeah, what about when that big cop...." In fact, we are gettin' downright chummy with 'em, but then the captain walks in.

All our talkin, stops when he appears, though he musta heard us long before we saw him, so there isn't really any point tryin' to pretend we have been this quiet all the time. Still, he doesn't look happy, so without any kind of spoken agreement we all drop back into our appointed roles. By this I mean the guards stand at parade rest and look stern, whilst me and Nunzio just sit and look uncomfortable... which isn't too hard since, as I said, we have not emerged from the fracas unscathed.

We watch in total silence as the captain sits down at his desk and starts studyin' the report which has been placed there. I suppose I could of looked at it myself when we was talkin' with the guards, but to tell you the truth it hadn't occurred to me until I see the captain readin' it and realize the fates of Nunzio and me might well be decided by what is in it.

Finally, the captain looks up as if seein' all of us for the first time.

"Where are the others?" he sez to one of the guards.

"At the infirmary tent, sir," the guard sez.

The captain raises his eyebrows.

"Anything serious?"

"No sir. Just a few bumps and bruises. Besides..."

The guard hesitates and glances at me, and I knew I was on.

"I told 'em they should get patched up and let me talk to you first, captain... sir," I sez. "You see, it was Nunzio and me what started the fight, and the squad just pitched in later to help us out... so I figured that... well, since we was responsible..."

"Can you verify this?" the captain sez to the guard, cuttin' my oration short.

"Yes sir."

"Very well. Send word over to the infirmary. Tell the rest of the squad they are free to return to their quarters after their wounds are treated. Sergeant Guido and Corporal Nunzio are taking full responsibility for their actions."

"Yes sir," the guard sez, then salutes and leaves.

This is a bit of a load off my mind, as I have been worryin' a bit about gettin' the crew into trouble with our gambit. A bit, but not all... as there remains the question of what the captain is gonna do about me and Nunzio. This is a for real question, as the stare the captain is levelin' at us is real noncommittal, which is to say he neither looks happy nor upset... though I'm not sure what he would have to be happy about in this situational.

"Are you aware," he sez finally, "that I was called off stage to deal with this matter? One song into my final set, no less?"

"No sir," I sez, 'cause I hadn't been.

This simple statement did, however, settle two things in my mind. First, there is the matter of his rather flashy outfit... which while it is

150

indeed quite spiffy, is decidedly non-regulation. Second, it removed any doubts I might be havin' as to the level of benevolence the captain is feelin' toward us... noncommittal stare or not.

"According to this," he sez, lookin' at the report again, "you two were involved in, if not the actual instigators of a barroom brawl, not only with civilians, but with the local police as well. Is there anything you'd like to add to that?"

"One of those civilians tried to roll one of our squad," I sez.

I figure that now we have accomplished our mission, it is time to start lookin' out for ourselves.

"Then, when we try to get him out, the others try to say he has assaulted her. As far as the cops... I mean, the local police go, well, they was tryin' to arrest us all, even though our own military police were right there on the scene of the alleged crime, and we was taught in basic trainin'..."

"Yes, yes, I know," he waves. "Soldiers are to be tried in military, not civilian court, so you two took on a whole room full of civilians over a point in the Military Code. Is that it?"

"Yes sir. That and to try to help one of our squad."

"Very well," he sez, and looks over at the guards. "You men can go now. I'll handle this from here."

We wait quite-like until the MPs file out of the room, then a little longer as the captain is studyin' our files again.

"You two have only been assigned to me for about a week... and only enlisted a few weeks before that. Is that correct?"

"Yes sir."

"So you're fresh out of Basic and already a sergeant... and corporal. And now this."

He goes back to starin' at our files, but I am startin' to feel a little less anxious. While there is no question of us beatin' the rap, as we have confessed, it's startin' to sound like we might get off with nothin' more than losin' our stripes... a possibility which does not distress me overly much. Not bad for not havin' a mouthpiece to do our plea bargainin'.

"The civilian authorities are recommending you be disciplined severely... that you be made an example of to discourage other soldiers from following your example."

I start feelin' anxious again. This does not sound so encouragin', and after a career unblemished by a single conviction, I am not eager to spend time in an army stockade. I wonder if it is too late to withdraw our confession... and whether the MPs are still outside.

"Very well," the captain sez finally, lookin' up from our files. "consider yourselves disciplined."

We wait for him to say more, then realize that's all there is.

"Sir?"

The captain gives a tight little smile at our reactions.

"Do you men know what an army that's growing as fast as our needs the most?"

I experience a sinkin' feelin' in my stomach, as I have heard this speech before. Nunzio, however, was not present the last time it was run past me.

"A better tailor," he sez.

The captain blinks in surprise, then erupts in a quick bark of laughter.

"That's pretty good," he sez. "A better tailor. You've got a point there, Corporal Nunzio... but that wasn't what I was referring to."

He drops his grin and gets back on track.

"What we need are leaders. You can train men to shoot, but you can't train them to lead. No really. We can show them the procedures and tell them the principles so they can at least go through the motions, but *real* leadership... the charisma to inspire loyalty and the guts to act in a crisis... that can't be taught."

He picks up the report and tosses it back down careless like.

"Now, publicly we have to discourage our soldiers from fighting with civilians, whatever the provocation. Any other position would endanger our welcome in the community... such as it is. We are aware, however, that there are those who try to exploit our men at any opportunity, and many who frankly resent us... though I never could understand why."

I am willin' to let this pass, but Nunzio doesn't.

"Maybe it's because the army is the major recipient of their tax money," he sez.

"But their taxes are being lowered, not increased by our campaigns," the captain frowns.

Just as it did the first time I heard it, this statement strikes an impure note in my mind. Again, however, I am not allowed time to pursue it.

"Whatever," the captain sez, shakin' his head. "The truth of the matter is, that while we cannot publicly condone incidents such as the one you were involved in, there are far worse

153

things in the army's eyes than to be willing to fight for your men *and* the Military Code. The fact that you were willing to take this stand against civilians, police even... and after only three weeks in army too... Tell me, have you men given any thought to going Career? Of making the army your permanent occupation?"

This takes us a little aback, as we have given this idea about the same consideration we would give pokin' ourselves in the eye with a sharp stick.

"Ummm... to be honest with you, sir," I manage at last, "we was gonna see how things worked out in our first tour of duty before tryin' to reach any decision."

This struck me as a diplomatic answer, as it is not wise to tell a man you think his career choice stinks on ice... especially when he is in a position of control over your immediate future. For some reason, however, the captain seems to take my response as an encouragin' sign.

"Perhaps I can make the decision a little easier for you," he sez, startin' to scribble in our files. "I'm promoting you both. Nunzio, you're a sergeant now... and Guido, you're getting another stripe. Of course, we can't have you wandering around town now... or your squad either, for that matter. It might get our civilian hosts upset. Tell you what. I'm going to transfer you and your squad to Headquarters Staff. There's always opportunity for advancement there. That's all, men. You can go now... and congratulations!"

*

I would like nothin' more than a little time to think over this latest development, but it is not to be. Nunzio barely waits until we are

154

clear of the commander's office before he starts on me.

"Guido," he sez, "am *I* crazy, or is the army?"

"Probably both," I sez, "though I'll admit I think the army has and edge on you in the 'foo-foo land' department."

"I don't get it. I just don't get it," he continues like I hadn't said anythin'. "I mean, we disobeyed standing orders... even roughed up the *cops* for cryin' out loud. And we get promoted for *that?*"

"It would seem," I sez carefully, "that we're bein' rewarded for 'action against the enemy.' I guess we just miscalculated who the army sees as 'the enemy,' is all."

We walk on in silence for a few, each of us reflectin' on what has occurred.

"I guess there is a good side to this," I sez at last. "If we are gonna continue our attempts to disrupt the army, headquarters is probably the best place to do it from."

"True enough," Nunzio sighs. "Well, Guido, let me be the first to congratulate you."

"On what?"

"Why, on your promotion, of course," he sez, glancin' sideways at me. "I know *exactly* how much it means to you."

I think of hittin' him, but he has deliberately stepped out of range as he lays this on me.

"Nunzio," I sez, "let us not forget your own..."

"Hey guys!! Wait up!!"

We look around to find Spyder comin' up behind us.

"Oh, hi Spyder."

"So what happened?" she sez, tryin' to get her wind back as she catches up to us.

"Well, there was a bit of a fight after you left, and..."

"I *know* that," she interrupts. "I heard. Sorry I missed it. I meant afterward. Are you guys in trouble?"

"Naw," Nunzio shrugs casual-like. "In fact, we're all being transferred to Headquarters Staff... oh yeah, and Guido and me got promoted."

He sez this real easy, expectin' her to be as surprised as we was. Strangely enough, however, she let's it skate on by her.

"What about the civilian authorities? What are you gonna do about them?"

"Nothin'," I sez. "Why should we?"

"Are you kidding? The way I heard it you punched out a cop! They aren't gonna just ignore *that*!"

"They're gonna have to," I shrugs. "As soldiers, we are subject to discipline by the military, *not* civilian courts."

"We are?" she frowns, stoppin' in her tracks.

"Sure. Don't you remember? They told us about that back in Basic."

"I *told* you you should pay attention to the Military Law lectures," Nunzio sez, grinnin' at her.

"Gee," she sez, chewin' her lip. "Then I guess you don't need the help I brought you."

"Help? What help?"

"Well, I thought you were gonna be in trouble with the civilian authorities, and since I knew you guys was connected, I figured I should find somebody to pass the word to so..."

Until now I had only been listenin' casually. As Spyder spoke, however, a loud alarm began to sound in the back of my mind... a *very* loud alarm.

"Connected?" I sez, interruptin'. "You mean like with the Mob?"

"Of course," she sez.

"You went lookin' for the Mob?" Nunzio sez, catchin' on at last.

"That's right. Found 'em, too."

"Wait a minute," I frowns. "When youse said you 'brought back help,' were you sayin' you've got somebody along *now?*"

"That's right," she sez, lookin' around. "He was with me when I spotted you a second ago. I may have gotten a little ahead of him, but he should..."

"Hello Guido... Nunzio... long time no see."

The owner of this new voice melts out of the shadows close to us... too close.

"Hello, Snake," I sez, edgin' a little away from Nunzio so we both have lots of room for whatever is gonna happen next.

"You remember me!" he sez, though his mockin' smile makes it clear he is not surprised. "I wasn't sure you would."

I don't think anyone would have trouble rememberin' Snake... except for maybe, witnesses... as he is what you would call highly memorable. He is tall and real thin, and has a habit of dressin' all in black like he is now, which is why he was able to ease up on us in the shadows.

"You guys know each other?" Spyder sez, hesitant-like lookin' back and forth between us.

"Oh, we're old friends," Snake sez in that smooth, purrin' voice of his.

"Actually, it's more like 'associates,' " Nunzio corrects, easin' even further apart from me.

While both Nunzio and me know Snake, we have never pretended to like him. He is one of the top enforcers for the Mob, but tends to like his work a little too much for our tastes. You have perhaps noticed that when the occasion calls for it, neither Nunzio nor me are adverse to the judicious application of violence, but as it goes against our delicate natures we have trained ourselves to terminate such encounters in the briefest possible time. Snake, on the other hand, likes to prolong and drag out his work as much as possible ...and he works with a knife. He can be as fast as his moniker when the situation calls for it, however, and though Nunzio and me had been confident about roustin' a room full of normal people earlier this evening, there is a serious question in my mind as to whether both of us workin' together can take Snake if things get ugly.

"Why don't you head on back to the barracks, Spyder," I sez, not takin' my eyes off Snake. "Our colleague here probably has some things he wants to discuss with us... privately."

"Not me!" Snake says, holdin' up his hands palm out in what to my eye is an exaggerated show of innocence. "...Though I'll admit I think a conversation between us would be... interesting. No, I'm just here to escort you to another old friend."

"And who would that be?" Nunzio sez.

Snake's smile slips away and his voice drops a dozen degrees.

"Don Bruce wants to talk to you... he wants to talk to you *real bad*."

Chapter 14

"You countermanded me on whose authority?"
Pope John

That's quite some babe you
got there."

I shoot a sideways glance at Snake when
he sez this, but his manner seems as respectful
as his tone, so I decide he is sincere and not
tryin' to be sarcastic.

"She's okay," I sez, noncommittal like.

Realizin' we are in trouble with the Mob, it
does not seem like the best idea to seem *too*
close to Spyder.

"So what happened to her hair?"

"I think she likes it that way," I shrugs.
"Who knows with broads. Of course, it looked
better before the army cropped it short."

"That reminds me of a joke I heard once,"
Nunzio sez. "It seems this guy takes an alliga-

tor, then cuts off it's nose and tail, and paints it yellow..."

"You know," Snake interrupts, "while we were looking for you, she was asking me about joining the Mob after her enlistment is over."

I realize now why Snake is bein' so talkative. He is checkin' politely to see if either Nunzio or me has any claim on Spyder... professionally or personally. This is understandable, for while I do not think he is afraid of us, every guy knows that messin' with another guy's moll--or, in the Mob, his recruit--is apt to be considered a challenge, so it is wisest to check things out carefully before proceedin'. While it is not exactly gettin' permission, havin' the courtesy to ask is a good way to avoid blunderin' into somethin; thereby avertin' hurt feelin's, not to mention needless bloodshed.

"She's got her own mind," I sez cautious like. "Of course, she was askin' me and Nunzio the same thing a week ago, so *we* was kinda figurin' to sponsor her if it came to that."

"Okay, got it," Snake nods. "Of course, that depends on where you guys are going to be in the future."

He sez this easy enough, but it is a cold reminder of the realities of our situational. He is actin' friendly, like has no grudge against us other than, perhaps, professional rivalry. There is no doubt in our minds, however, that if Don Bruce gives him the word to whack us, he will do his best to carry out that order.

"Speaking of our future," Nunzio sez, "where are we going?"

I have a pretty good idea of the answer from the direction we have been walkin', and Snake confirms it.

"Back to Abdul's Sushi Bar and Bait Shop," he sez. "Or, as Guido here would say, the scene of the perpetration."

"Snake," I sez, drawin' myself up a little, "are you tryin' to make fun of the way I talk?"

"Me?" he sez, all innocent like. "Heavens no. I've always admired your command of the language, Guido, as does everyone else in the Mob I know. Besides..."

We have reached the doorway of our goal, but he pauses briefly to finish his sentence.

"I... *certainly* wouldn't want to offend anyone as tough as you... or you either, Nunzio. By the way, I *love* your new outfits. They really show off your legs, know what I mean?"

Now, I have been expectin' some kinda wisecrack about our uniforms ever since Snake stepped out of the shadows. It is oblivious to me, however, why he has waited until now to mouth off, as it allows him to duck through the door before we can reply by beatin' his head in... which is exactly what he does, leavin' us little choice but to follow him in.

"There they are now. Come in, boys! Come in!"

The scene which greets us can be taken in at a glance, but what that glance shows is none too promisin'.

The place is a wreck, with overturned and broken tables and chairs scattered everywhere. I had known we made a bit of a mess in the course of the altercation I mentioned earlier, but whilst it was in progress my attention was much more occupied with inflictin' damage on *people* whilst avoidin' receivin' damage from the same, so I had not been takin' close note of what was happenin' to the place itself. Lookin'

at it now without the distractin' activity, however, it is clear that housekeepin' is gonna have
their work cut out for them.

Don Bruce is leanin' against the bar
drinkin' wine from one of the few remainin'
bottles... drinkin' directly from the bottle as
there are no unbroken glasses remainin' that I
can see. Though his greetin' was real friendly,
there is no pretendin' that this is a social call,
as scattered around the room, leanin' against
the wall in the absence of chairs, is no less
than half a dozen Mob goons.

"Hi guys! Come join us!"

This comes from Tananda who is standin;
on one side of Don Bruce. She has dumped her
disguise for the occasion, but is wrapped in
Don Bruce's lavender coat. While he maybe
doesn't care for females the way Nunzio and me
do, Don Bruce is always the finest of gentlemen
when it comes to dealin' with them. Standin'
next to him on the other side, is...

"That's the ones! Those are the guys that
busted up the place! I thought I was paying you
for *protection!!"*

Frumple is there. For a minute I think he's
dropped his disguise as well, but then I realize
that he's still disguised as a local and that his
face is bright red 'cause he's hoppin' mad.

"All right, *all right!"* Don Bruce sez,
soundin' a little annoyed. "We'll consider that a
firm identification. Just get your place fixed up
and send us the bill... better still, give us a list
of what you need in supplies and repairs. We
can maybe get you some *discounts* from the
distributors and contractors... know what I
mean?"

"I should think so," Frumple snorts,

reachin' for the wine bottle.

"In the meantime," Don Bruce sez, movin' the bottle out of his reach, "why don't you take a little walk or something. There are a few things I want to discuss with the boys here."

The Deveel hesitates for a second, then nods his agreement.

"All right," he sez, but he shoots us a black look as he starts for the door. "I should have known that double-crossing Skeeve was behind you two... I suspected it from the start. Him and this floozie of his..."

"Hold it!!"

Don Bruce's voice cracked through the place like a whip, and I knew Frumple had made a mistake... a bad mistake.

"What did you just say about Skeeve? ...And Miss Tananda here?"

The goons have come off the wall and are startin' to drift forward.

"I... um... that is..." the Deveel sez, lookin' around desperate-like.

"Perhaps you should consider being a bit more careful in your selection of words when describing an associate of mine... *or* a lady who is a personal friend *and* present at the time."

"Well... you see..." Frumple tries, but the Don isn't finished yet.

"I've reconsidered my settlement offer," he sez. "I don't think that fixin' this place up again will do... considering the damage to your reputation. I think we'll have to set you up in a whole new place."

This confuses the Deveel, but he is scared enough to remember his manners.

"That's nice of you," he sez. "But I don't think..."

164

"...On Deva!" Don Bruce sez, droppin' the other shoe.

For a second Frumple's eyes snap wide open. Then he turns on us like a cornered rat.

"You... you gave me your word!" he screeches. "You said you wouldn't tell anyone..."

"They didn't have to tell me nothin'," Don Bruce snaps. "I got ears in a lot of places... *includin'* the Bazaar."

"But I can't go back there!"

"I know that, too," Don Bruce sez cold-like. "Still, that's our offer. Either we set you up on Deva... *or* you stay right here and pay for your own repairs. Take it or leave it."

Now, I hadn't known that Don Bruce knew that Frumple was a Deveel, just like I was unaware that the Deveel was unwelcome in his own dimension for some reason. My surprise, however, was nothin' compared to Frumple's reaction. He looks like he's in shock.

"I... I can't go back there," he manages to repeat, finally.

"Good. Then it's settled." Don Bruce is suddenly friendly again. "Now why don't you go ahead and take that walk... and by the way..."

The Deveel turns to find the Don starin' at him real hard- like.

"...Remember what I said... I got ears in a lot of places. If you start runnin' off at the mouth, *or* do anything to give Skeeve, Miss Tananda, or the boys here any grief, I'll hear about it. Remember that. Now, get outta here."

Frumple slinks off, and as soon as he's gone, Don Bruce jerks his head at the goons.

"You boys take a walk, too," he sez. "What we got to talk about is private... and Snake?"

"Yes, Boss?"

"Keep an eye on that joker, will you? Make sure he doesn't talk to anyone... 'cause if he tries, I'm afraid he might have a little accident. Know what I mean?"

"Got it, Boss," Snake says, and follows the others out into the night.

"Well, boys," Don Bruce sez, turnin' to us at last. "Now that we're alone, I think it's about time we had us a little talk."

He is real friendly as he says this, but as you yourselves can see from the preceedin' incident with Frumple, this is not as reassurin' as it would appear. It occurs to me that I would not like to sit in on a Dragon Poker game with Don Bruce, as he would doubtless make you a friendly loan so's you could keep playin' while at the same time havin' a whole extra deck of cards hidden in his lap.

"Miss Tananda here was just tellin' me about your current operation..."

"That's right," Tananda sez. "Don Bruce didn't..."

"...and realizing, as you have just heard, that I pride myself in being informed," the Don continues, talkin' right over Tananda... which is a bad sign, "it was a little embarrassing to have to admit my ignorance until your little friend came to me this evening for help. Now, what I want to know is..."

"What are you doing operating in the kingdom of Possiltum... especially considering the agreement we made?"

"Agreement?" Tananda sez in a small voice.

"That's right," Don Bruce sez, turnin' to her. "you weren't around at the time, but way back when I first met Skeeve, we made a deal and I gave him my personal word that the Mob wouldn't move on the kingdom of Possiltum."

"But what does that..."

"...and since Skeeve... and through him, all of you... are now on the Mob's payroll as employees, *your presence here is breakin' my word. Capish?*"

"I see," Tananda sez, glancin' over at us with new understandin'. "But tell me, Don Bruce, if the Mob isn't operating in this kingdom, then what are you doing taking protection money from merchants like Frumple? In fact, what are you doing here at all?"

This is a good question, and one which has not occurred to me... though I suspect I know the answer. The Don has enough grace to look a little embarrassed, though, when he gives it.

"All this if from *before* I gave my word," he sez. "I never said we was going to give up the operations we already had in place."

"Hmmm..." Tananda frowns, "it sounds like a pretty fine distinction to me."

Of course, the Mob makes a lot of money from such fine distinctions... but this does not seem like the time to bring it up.

"That may be," Don Bruce sez, his voice hardenin' up again. "But it's beside the point. I'm still waiting to hear what *you're* doing here!"

"Oh that," Tananda smiles. "Well, you see... umm..."

Though Tananda is no slouch at Dragon Poker and is actin' very confident, I can see she is stuck and trying to bluff.

"Relax, Tananda," Nunzio sez, speakin' for the first time since we came in. "I can explain it."

"You can?" I sez, slippin' a bit in my surprise.

"Sure," my cousin insists, lookin' at me hard like he does when I'm supposed to be ready to provide him with an alibi.

"All right, Nunzio," Don Bruce sez, settlin' back against the bar, "start talking."

"Well, you see, Don Bruce," Nunzio sez, "the Boss is unhappy with the agreement you referenced regarding the Mob's relationship with Possiltum."

"Oh he is, is he?" the Don snarls, but Nunzio holds up a hand and continues.

"The way it is," he sez, "is the Boss figures that circumstances have arisen which *neither* of you took into account in the original negotiation... specifically, the new expansion policy that's pushing the borders out."

"Go on," Don Bruce sez, but he's nodding now.

"The *spirit* of your agreement was that the Mob wouldn't infringe on the kingdom's territory, but the way it's going, the *kingdom* is pushing into the *Mob's* territory. What's more, the *letter* of your agreement is keeping the Mob from protecting what's ours."

"So I noticed," the Don sez, sarcastic-like.

"Now, the Boss doesn't think this is right. What's more *he* feels personally responsible since it was his sloppy negotiating for the kingdom that has placed you in this predicament. The problem is that as he is now working for the Mob and not for the kingdom, he is not in a position to renegotiate the terms to make things right again."

"Yeah," Don Bruce sez thoughtful like, "I can see that."

"Now, you may not know it, Don Bruce,"

Nunzio continues, "but the Boss thinks the world of you and would never do anything to hurt you or your reputation. Because of this, and because he feels responsible for your current difficulties, he has taken it upon himself to correct the situation by mounting a covert operation to halt the kingdom's expansion. In fact, the reason he has been keeping this secret from you is for a little extra insurance. This way, if anything goes wrong, you can swear under oath that you knew nothing about it, and certainly never took a hand or gave an order against Possiltum. What he's doing, Don Bruce, is setting himself up to be a scapegoat... all to take the pressure off you!"

While I am occasionally less than complimentary when referrin' to Nunzio's long-winded tendencies, there are times when I am truly grateful for his talent for shovelin'... like now. Even bein' as aware as I am of the truth of the matter, that the Boss has probably overlooked his agreement with Don Bruce completely when givin' us this assignment, I am not sure I could separate fact from guff in my cousin's rendition, even with the aid of a pry bar.

"That Skeeve!" Don Bruce laughs, hittin' the bar with his fist in his enthusiasm. "Can you see why I love him? He's really trying to do all this on his own... just for me? I'll tell you, boys..."

He glances around, then hunches forward before continuin'.

'You have no idea how much grief the other Mob bosses have been giving me because of that agreement. Especially the boss of the Island Mob."

"You mean Don Ho?" I sez.

"That's right," Don Bruce nods. "Even the boss of the senior citizens' Mob... Don Amechie! They've all been on my case. I'm just surprised that Skeeve was aware of it. I keep telling you, that boy's got real promise. You know what an organization as big as ours needs the most?"

"Leadership," Nunzio and me answer at the same time.

"Lead... Hey! That's right!" the Don sez, blinkin' at us in surprise. "You know, you boys have been shaping up pretty well yourselves since you started working for Skeeve. Maybe I should start giving some thought to setting you up with your own operations."

It occurs to me that this promotion thing is gettin' totally out of hand.

"Ummm... We're pretty happy with things the way they are, Don Bruce," I sez, quick-like.

"Yeah," Nunzio chimes in. "We figure the way things are going, the Boss is gonna need all the help we can give him."

"Hmmm... I suppose you're right," the Don sez, makin' us both a little uncomfortable with how unwillin' he seems to give up the idea of advancin' us in the ranks. "Tell you what, though, like Skeeve says, I can't taken an open hand in this thing you got going, but if you want I can assign a few boys to give you a hand!"

A picture flits across my mind. A picture of me tryin' to sleep, much less operate, with Snake loiterin' about in the near vicinity.

"I... don't think so," I sez. "We're pretty used to workin' with the crew we got already. Besides, any of the boys you assigned to us would have to enlist... and there's no guarantee where they'd get assigned."

"...And most of them would quit before they'd be seen in public in those outfits you're wearing," Don Bruce laughs, winkin' at Tananda. "Yeah. You got a point."

Me and Nunzio force smiles, which is as close as we can manage to joining in the merriment.

"Well, be sure to let me know if there's anything I can do to help."

"Sure, Don Bruce."

"Thanks, Don Bruce."

"Oh yeah! One more thing. How's Bunny doing?"

"Bunny?" Tananda sez, comin' off the bar like a prizefighter. "That little..."

"Sure! You remember Bunny," I interrupts quick like. "Don Bruce's *niece* who's workin' with us?"

"Oh! Right!" Tananda blinks, and settles back again.

"She's working out real well, Don Bruce," Nunzio supplies hurriedly. "In fact, right now she's holding down our office while we're out in the field."

"Yeah, right," Don Bruce waves. "But how is she getting along with Skeeve?"

Even though we can maybe snow him from time to time, the Don is pretty quick, and he catches our hesitation and glances at Tananda.

"Say... *you* aren't interested in Skeeve yourself, are you, Miss Tananda?"

Tananda thinks for a second, then wrinkles her nose.

"Not really," she sez. "I guess he's kind of like a kid brother to me."

"I see," Don Bruce nods. "Well, as a favor to me, could you take Bunny under your wing, too? She likes to talk tough and comes on like she's real experienced and worldly, but inside she's still just a kid. Know what I mean?"

In response, Tananda just nods slow-like. To my eye, she seems less than thrilled with the idea... especially after hearin' how serious Don Bruce takes promises.

"You know how the Boss is when it comes to dames," I sez, quick-like. "Slower'n a bail bondsman what's been stung three times runnin'."

I am tryin' to draw attention away from Tananda, but the Don is ignorin' me and starin' at her instead.

"Say... are you okay?" he sez, misreadin' her signals. "It looks like you've been takin' more than your share of lumps in this operation."

"I'm just a little tired," she sez, flashin' a quick smile. "You're right, though. I'm not getting any younger, and I'm not sure how many more nights like this I can take."

"Why don't you head on back to Big Julie's and hook up with Chumley?" I sez. "We're gettin' transferred out of here, and there's not much you'll be able to do on your own realizin' the shape you're in."

"Transferred?"

"That's right," Nunzio sez. "We've been promoted and transferred to headquarters. It seems the Mob isn't the only ones who can spot leadership potential."

As an indication of the physical and nervous stress of the night we have been through, I do not have the energy to even *think* about throttlin' him.

Chapter 15

"An army travels on its paperwork!"
J. Carlson

Well, Sergeant Guido, you and your squad come highly recommended. Yes, highly recommended indeed!"

"Yes, sir. Thank you, sir."

Okay, so I am layin' it on a little thick. Considerin' the number of officers I'm seein' here at headquarters, however, it seems like the wisest attitude for an enlisted type like me to assume... which is to say one step up from grovelin'.

"Well," he sez, settin' our files to one side and startin' to rummage through the other stacks of paper on his desk, "let's see what we can find for you in the way of assignments."

Actually, I would be surprised if he can find his *feet* in this office. It has only been a few times that I have seen so much paper stuffed into as little space as there is in this office... and most of the other times was in the offices I poked into while lookin' for this one. There is paper stacked *everywhere*, on the chairs and on the floor, on the window ledges and on the tops of file cabinets... not to mention the stacks set on the top of already filed paper in the open drawers of said cabinets. There are also, of course, assorted piles of paper on the desktop of the officer I am speakin' to, and it is through these stacks he is currently rummagin'.

"Ah! Here's something," he sez, pausin' to peer at one of the sheets he has been rifflin' through. "What would you say to my assigning you and your crew as sanitation engineers."

"As what?"

"You know," he sez, "digging and filling latrines."

It occurs to me that while there might be *some* potential for disruptin' the army from such a position, it is not a route I would be particularly eager to take. You see, Nunzio still ribs me about my work with the Realistic Doggie Doodle with Lifelike Aroma that Actually Sticks to Your Hands on my last assignment for M.Y.T.H. Inc., and I would therefore prefer to avoid workin' with variations on the real thing this time around.

"It sounds like a stinkin' detail... sir," I sez, the words sort of slippin' out.

I try to recover by addin' "...if you'll forgive the play on words...sir."

That's so he'll know I read.

I expect him to get a bit upset at my forthrightness, but instead he just gives a little shrug.

"Of course it is," he sez with refreshin' honesty. "But remember where you are, Sergeant. This is Headquarters... the brains of the army. It only stands to reason that most of that brain power is devoted to finding nicer, cushier assignments for the owners of those brains... which is to say the place is armpit deep in politics... if I make myself clear."

"Not really, sir."

The officer sighs.

"Let me try to explain it this way. Here, everybody knows somebody, and uses their connections to get the best jobs. The higher the connections, the better the jobs. You and your squad, on the other hand, have just arrived and consequently know nobody... which means that for a while, you'll have to content yourselves with the jobs no one else wants. I expect that as you make connections, you'll get better duties, but for the time being that's the way it is."

I consider mentionin' my connections with the Mob, but decide they will be of little value in this circumstantial and may even be construed as a threat. Then something else occurs to me.

"Is General Badaxe available, sir?"

This gets the officer's attention.

"You know General Badaxe?" he sez from under sky-high eyebrows.

"Not to any great extent, sir," I admit. "We just met once in passin'."

"Oh. Well, he *is* here at Headquarters, of course. I think you'll find that he's indisposed, however... at least he has been for the last couple of weeks."

"Would that indisposition by any chance be

female, sir? Extra, extra large... a lot of makeup and jewelry?"

This earns me a lot harder look from the officer before he answers.

"As a matter of fact, yes," he sez at last. "You seem remarkably well informed for someone who has just arrived at Headquarters... or do you know the... young lady as well?"

For several reasons I figure it would be wisest *not* to admit the true relationship Nunzio and me has with Massha.

"She was with the general when I met him at court, sir," I sez, sorta truthfully.

"You've been to the Royal Court?"

"Yes sir... but it was a while back... just before the king married Queen Hemlock."

"I see," the officer sez, thoughtful-like, then sets the paper he was holdin' aside and starts rummagin' again.

"Well in that case, perhaps I *can* find something a bit more pleasant in the way of an assignment.

"Take your time sir," I sez. "I can understand how things can be a bit disorganized with the general gone so much."

"Not really," the officer sez, absentminded-like. "If anything, they're going smoother."

"Excuse me? ...sir?"

"What? Oh," he sez, returnin' his concentration to the situational at hand. "Well, I probably shouldn't say anything, but since you already know some of the personalities involved..."

He pauses to glance around like some one might be loiterin' among the stacks of paper... which considerin' their height is a real possibility.

"If you know General Badaxe, then you probably already know that while he is a more than adequate leader, he is rather inflexible in his attitudes as to how things should be done. That is, he wants things done *his* way, whether there is a better way of doing things or not."

This description sounds like everyone in the army I've met above the rank of corporal, but I content myself with noddin' in agreement.

"Well, a lot of us officers who came on board during the current expansion drive originally served under Big Julie back when he led the invasion of Possiltum. In some ways it's nice because it guaranteed us rank in the Possiltum army, but it also means we know there are other ways of doing things than the way General Badaxe wants... lots better ways. The trouble is, until now we haven't been able to implement any changes or improvements without disobeying orders from the general."

"And now?" I urge, not even botherin' to add a 'sir' to it.

"Now, with the general 'indisposed,'" the officer smiles, gettin' a little lost in his own thoughts, "we're left pretty much on our own, which means we get to do things *our* way for a change. If Badaxe stays out of our hair for another few weeks, we should have this army whipped into shape so we can *really* get down to business. I'll tell you, serving under Big Julie might have been a pain from time to time, but that man sure knows how to run an army. I wonder how he's doing now that he's retired?"

"Last time I saw him, he was doin' great."

If I had said God himself was walkin' through the door I couldn't have gotten a bigger reaction from the officer. He sits up straight sudden-like, and his eyes lose their dreamy focus and center on me... though I notice they are buggin' out a little.

"You know Big Julie?" he sez in kind of a reverent whisper. "When was the last time you talked with him?"

"A couple weeks back," I sez. "Just before Nunzio and me enlisted. "We was sippin' some wine with him and some friends over at his villa."

"You were a guest at his villa? Tell me, is it..."

The officer breaks off and shakes his head like a dog.

"Excuse me, sergeant," he sez, in much more normal tones. "I didn't mean to pry. It's just that... well, Big Julie is something of a legend around Headquarters. I was a junior officer when I served under him, and never met him personally... just saw him a couple of times during reviews and inspections."

"That's too bad," I sez, with real sympathy. "He's really a great guy. You'd like him... sir."

I finally remembers I was talkin' to an officer, and my 'sir' seemed to remind him of why I was in his office in the first place.

"Now that I think of it," he sez, pullin' some papers off the top of one of his stacks, "there *is* something here that I could assign you and your crew to. Would you like to take over running one of our supply depots?"

This sounds like just what we need to do the most damage to the army's attempts to reorganize. I also notice that the officer is now *askin'* me about which assignment I want.

"That sounds fine, sir."

"Good," he sez, startin' to scribble on the

179

sheets. "We have a whole supply crew in the infirmary right now--got a bad batch of chili or something. Anyway, I'll just put you and your squad in there as replacements, and when they get out, they can take the sanitation engineer slots."

It occurs to me that these other guys are gonna be less than thrilled with their new assignment, but that, of course, is not my problem. Still, it will be a good idea if for a while we keep a lookout for anyone tryin' to sneak up on us from the downwind side.

"Thank you sir," I sez, and mean it.

"Just report to Supply Depot Number Thirteen and you'll be all set."

"Yes sir... ummm... is it far? I mean, I got my crew outside and we got all our gear with us..."

"Just flag down one of the wagons going your way and hitch a ride," he sez. "One of the nicer things about working at Headquarters... with the supply depots right here is that there are *lots* of wagons around. You'll rarely have to walk anywhere."

"Yes sir. Thank you again, sir."

"Oh... Sergeant Guido?"

"Sir?" I sez, turnin' back to him.

He is pushin' a stack of papers across his desk toward me that must weigh more than twenty pounds.

"Since you'll be riding, you might as well take this with you instead of waiting for it to be delivered by courier."

"I... I don't understand, sir," I sez, eyein' this mountain of dead weight suspiciously like it was a distant relative arrivin' unannounced. "Do you want I should store this for you over at

180

the depot?"

"Of course not," the officer sez, givin' a little laugh. "This is for your requisition and inventory forms."

I am likin' this less and less the more I hear.

"You mean we gotta fill all this out just to move somethin' in or out of the depot... sir?"

"You misunderstand me, sergeant," he sez quick like. "These aren't the forms themselves."

I experience a quick flood of relief.

"...These are just the *instructions* for filling out the forms!"

The relief I had been feelin' disappears like a single shot of whiskey in a big bowl of watered-down punch.

"The instructions," I echoes weakly, starin' at the pile.

All of a sudden this assignment is not lookin' as good as it had a few minutes ago.

The officer notices the expression on my face.

"Come, come now, sergeant," he sez, givin' me what I guess is supposed to be a fatherly smile. "It's not as bad as it looks."

"It isn't?"

"No. It's really quite simple once you get the hang of it. Just read these instructions all the way through, then follow everything they say to the letter, and everything will be fine."

"If you say so, sir," I sez, unconvinced.

"Yes, I *do* say so... *sergeant*," he sez, givin' up his sales effort. "I *told* you we were going to get things under control and to do that, proper documentation is vital. It may look like a lot of needless hassle, but believe me, unless all the paperwork for supplies is filled out correctly,

182

the best of armies will bog down and become ineffective."

"Yes sir. Thank you, sir."

With that, I salute and get out of his office quick... takin' the stack of paper with me, of course. All of a sudden, my depression over seein' the massive list of instructions disappears. Instead, I am feelin' a degree of optimism I have not felt since the Boss sent us on this assignment without realizin' what he was doin', the officer has just made our job a lot easier.

"Without proper paperwork," he had said, "the army will bog down and cease to be effective..." and, as you know, the effectiveness of the army was a matter of no small concern to me and Nunzio.

Chapter 16

*"So what's wrong with following
established procedures?"*
M. Gorbachev

The warehouse which was
Supply Depot Number Thirteen was truly im-
mense, which is to say it was big. In fact, it was
so huge that youse got the feelin' that if the
weather turned bad, they could move all the
stuff out of here and have the war indoors. The
only trouble with that idea was that by the time
they got everythin' moved out, odds are they
would have forgotten what it was they was
fightin' about in the first place... but even if
they could remember, they'd probably be too
tired to want to fight about it.

There was racks of stuff everywhere, with
aisles big enough to drive a wagon down scattered around so as to carve everythin' into a
series of islands, and *lots* of tunnels and

crawlspaces twistin' their way into each of the islands. I occurred to me upon first viewin' this expanse that it was gonna be a perfect base of operation for us, as when and if anythin' went wrong, it would make one whale of a hideout. This thought was amplified when we discovered that the crew what had worked here before us had apparently opted to live on-site, as there were a lot of "nests" and hole-ups around the warehouse furnished with cots and hammocks and pillows and other stuff obliviously filched from the piles of supplies.

In short, it was a sweet setup, and the crew loses no time settlin' in, after some of them scattered and went explorin' to find out just what sort of stuff we have inherited to ride herd on while a couple of us tried to make sense out of the paperwork and charts heaped up on the desks.

"Hoo-ey!" Shu Flie sez, emergin' from the stacks with his brother at his side. "I've never seen so much stuff in one place! They got everything here!"

"A lot of it's pretty old, though," Hy Flie sez. "We had newer stuff than some of this junk back on the farm... and most of that stuff is still around from Pop Flie."

"Pop Flie?" I sez before I has a chance to think about whether or not I really wants to hear the answer.

"That's our grandpa," Shu explains. "Course, sometimes we call him..."

"I get the picture," I sez, interruptin' before he can explain any more.

It occurs to me to make a point of *not* ever visitin' the Flie residence.

"What I can't figure," Junebug sez, joinin'

our discussion, "is how they keep track of all this stuff. I mean, there doesn't seem to be any order or scheme to how things are stored. It's like they just keep pushing the old pile further back and stack the new stuff in front as it comes in without any effort to group things by category."

This sounds uncomfortably like the beginnin' of an idea which could improve our efficiency... which is, of course, the last thing my cousin and me want to see happen. Sneakin' a glance at Nunzio, I can see he's thinkin' the same thing, and catchin' my eye he gives a little shake of his head to confirm that observational.

"Ummm... I don't guess it is such a bad system, Junebug," I sez, thinkin' fast. "I mean, would *you* want to rearrange all this stuff to make room for each new shipment as it comes in?"

"You could get around that by leaving extra room in each storage category," he sez, not backin' off from his idea. "We gotta do *something* to organize this mess. Otherwise, we'll be spending all our time just trying to locate each item when we have to fill an order. I can't see how they've been operating around here without some kind of system."

"They've got a system all right," Spellin' Bee sez, lookin' up from the Forms Instruction Manual he was readin'. "The problem is, they've got so much duplicate paperwork to fill out they probably never had any time left over to try to organize the warehouse itself! I can't believe they expect us to fill out all these forms for every item in and out of inventory."

What the officer told me flashes across my

mind, and it gives me an idea.

"Do you think you can come up with a better trackin' system, Bee?" I sez.

"Probably," he sez, shuttin' the instruction manual. "Let's see... we'd need some sort of floor map... two of them actually, one so we know what's already here and where it is, and a second to establish the redefined areas... and then a simple In/Out Log so we could track the movement of items..."

"Okay," I interrupts, "get started on it. Figure out what we're gonna have to do and what you'll need in the way of information."

This, of course, earns me a hard look from Nunzio.

"I... If you say so, Guido," Bee sez, hesitantly, glancin' at the instruction manual. "But shouldn't we be following the established procedures?"

"Just go ahead and work up your plan," I sez. "We'll worry about fillin' out the army paperwork *after* we get this place functionin' the way we think it should."

"Okay," Bee shrugs. "Come here a second, guys, and I'll show you what I need. If you can start mapping out what's already here, I can start roughing out an In/Out Log, and..."

"Excuse me, *Sergeant* Guido," Nunzio sez. "Can I have a word with you... in private?"

"Why certainly, *Sergeant* Nunzio," I smile, givin' it right back to him, and follow him as he moves a little ways away from where the crew is huddlin'.

"What are you trying to do?" he hisses, as soon as we are alone. "Maybe I missed a loop, but I was under the impression that improving efficiency was the *last* thing we wanted to do here!"

"It is," I sez, "except everyone on the crew is thinkin' just the opposite. I'm just stallin' for a little time by insistin' that Bee come up with a complete plan before we actually have to *implement* any changes."

"Okay," Nunzio nods, "but what happens after he finishes comin' up with a new set up?"

"Then we either stall some more... *or* see if things will actually get fouled up more if we go ahead and try to go against army procedures. The officer what was briefin' me seemed pretty certain that the whole army will grind to a halt if all that paperwork Bee is talkin' about doesn't get filled out. At the very least we should have a chance to find out whether or not he is right."

"I dunno," my cousin frowns, "It seems to me that..."

"Guido! Nunzio!!"

We turn to find an apparition bearin' down on us. At first, I think it is one of those new armored wagons the army has been experimentin' with... only done up as a parade float. Then I look again, and see that it's...

"Massha!"

By the time I get this out, our associate has reached us, wrappin' one meaty arm around each of us in a humongous hug.

"I *heard* you guys were here and just *had* to come by and say 'Hi'!"

Because I am sorta to one side of her instead of directly in front of her, I can see past her to where our crew has stopped what they are doin' to gape at us... which is the normal reaction of folks what is seen' Massha for the first time.

188

"H...Hi, Massha," Nunzio sez, managin' to squirm loose. "How are things going? Any word from the Boss?"

"Not a peep," Massha sez, lettin' go of me. "There were some funny signs coming through a while back on the monitor ring I gave him, but they settled down and since then everything seems to be normal."

Do you think he's okay?" I sez. "He's been gone nearly three weeks now."

"Maybe... maybe not," she shrugs. "Remember that time doesn't flow at the same speeds on all dimensions. It may only have been a few *days* where he is."

"I get it," Nunzio nods solemn-like. "Like in Moorcock's *Eternal Champion* books."

"That's right," Massha beams. "As to your other question, things couldn't be going better. Hugh and I are hitting it off like a house afire. I'll tell you boys, I don't like to brag, but I've got him so lovesick, I don't think he remembers that he's *in* the army... much less that he's supposed to be running it."

Now, I haven't read the book they was chattin' about a second ago, but this is somethin' I *can* comment on.

"Ummm... Massha?" I sez. "That may not be such a good thing."

"What do you mean?" she sez, her smile fadin' as she looks back and forth between Nunzio and me. "That was my assignment, wasn't it?"

"Tell her, Guido," Nunzio sez, dumpin' the job of givin' Massha the bad news in my lap.

"Well, the way *I'm* hearin' it," I sez, wishin' I was dead or otherwise preoccupied, "the army is functionin' better without him."

"But that doesn't make sense!"

"It does when you consider that the layer of officers directly under him trained and served under Big Julie," Nunzio sez, redeemin' himself by coming' to my rescue. "The more you keep him away from his troops, the more those officers get to run things their way... and it seems they're better at this soldierin' than General Badaxe is."

"So you're saying that the best thing I could do to louse up things is to let Hugh go back to commanding the army?" Massha sez, chewin' her lower lip thoughtful-like. "Is that it?"

"So it would seem," I sez, relieved at not havin' to be the first to voice this logical conclusion. "I'm really sorry, Massha."

She heaves a hugh sigh, which on her is really somethin', then manages a wry grin.

"Oh well," she sez. "It was fun while it lasted. Nice to know I can still distract a man when I set my mind to it, though."

Politeness and self-preservation convince me to refrain from makin' any editorial additions to this comment.

"I guess I'll just say my goodbyes and head back to Big Julie's," she continues. "Any word from the other team?"

"They've called it quits, too," Nunzio sez. "You'll probably see them when you get to Big Julie's and they can fill you in on the details."

"So it's all riding on the two of you, huh?" she sez, cocking an eyebrow at us. "Well, good luck to you. I'd better get moving and let you get back to work. It looks like your friends are waiting for you."

I glance over where she is lookin' and sure

enough, the whole crew is standin' there, alternately glancin' at us and mutterin' together.

Wavin' goodbye to Massha, we ambles over to join them.

"Who was that?" Spyder sez, kinda suspicious-like.

"Who, that?" I sez, tryin' to make it casual. "Oh, just an old friend of ours."

"Scuttlebutt has it that she's the general's girlfriend," Junebug sez in a flat voice.

"Where'd you hear that?" Nunzio sez, innocent-like.

"Here and there," Junebug shrugs. "Face it, there can't be many people around Headquarters who would fit her description."

He had us there.

"Isn't it about time you guys told us exactly what is going on?" Spellin' Bee sez.

I realize, far too late, that we have been seriously underestimatin' the intelligence of our crew.

"What do you mean by that?" Nunzio sez, still tryin' to bluff his way out of it.

"Come on, Nunzio," Junebug sighs, "it's been pretty obvious since Basic that you and Guido here don't really belong in the army. You've got too much going for you to pass yourselves off as average recruits."

"You fight too good and shoot too good for someone who's supposed to be learnin' all this for the first time," Shu Flie sez.

"...And you've got too many connections in high places," Spyder adds, "like with the Mob."

"...And with devils," Bee supplies.

"...And now with the general's girlfriend," Junebug finishes. "All we want to know is, what are you guys *really* doing in the army? I mean, I suppose it's none of our business, but as long as we're servin' together, what affects you affects us."

"Bee here thinks you're part of some secret investigation team," Hy Flie sez, "and if that's what's going on we'll try to help... unless it's us you're supposed to be investigating."

"Well, guys," Nunzio sez, shakin' his head, "I guess you found us out. Bee's right. You see, the army wants us to..."

"No," I sez, quiet like.

Nunzio shoots me a look, but keeps goin'.

"What Guido means is we aren't supposed to talk about it, but since you've already..."

"I said 'No,' Nunzio!" I sez, squarin' off with him. "The crew's been playin' it straight with us all along. *I* say it's time we told them the truth... the *real* truth."

Nunzio hesitates, as he is not real eager to go head to head with me, then glances back and forth between me and the crew.

"Okay," he sez finally. "It's your funeral... go ahead and tell them."

Then he leans against the desk with his arms folded while I fill the crew in on our assignment... startin' with how the Boss's plan to keep Queen Hemlock from tryin' to take over the world fell apart when King Rodrick died, right up to our current plans to try to use our position in the supply depot to mess up the army's progress. They're all real quiet while I'm talkin', and even when I'm done no one sez anythin' for a long time.

"Well," sez Spyder, breakin' the silence, "the way I see it, we can't mess up *every* shipment or the army will just jerk us out of here. We'd better hold it down to one in five for a while."

"One in ten would be better," Junebug sez. "Otherwise..."

"Wait a minute! Stop the music! Nunzio explodes, interruptin' the conversation. "Are you guys sayin' you're willin' to *help* us screw things up?"

"Sure. Why not?" Shu Flie sez, puttin' a hand on my shoulder. "You and the Swatter here have been lookin' out for us since Basic. It's about time we did something for you for a change."

"Besides," his brother chimes in, "it's not like you're trying to bring down the kingdom or destroy the army. You're just out to slow things up a little... and that's fine by us."

"What it boils down to," Spyder smiles, "is that after working with you two all this time, we know you well enough to trust you to not hurt us... or anyone else for that matter... unless it's absolutely necessary. I think I speak for all of us when I say we've got no problem putting our support behind any plan you think is right. Am I right, guys?"

There is a round of nods and affirmative grunts, but I am only half payin' attention. It is occurrin' to me that I am buildin' a better understandin' of what the Boss means when he sez he's nervous about commandin' more loyalty than he deserves. While the crew is sayin' they don't believe we would do anythin' to hurt them, I am thinkin' about how we set them up for the barroom fight in Twixt... a detail I omitted when I was testifyin' about our recent activities. This makes me feel a little low, and while I am not about to refuse their help, I find it strengthens my resolve to avoid such leadership and decision makin' positions in the future.

"What about you, Bee?" Nunzio is sayin', "you aren't lookin' too happy. You want out?"

"N...No. It isn't that," Bee sez, quick-like. "I'm willing to help as much as I can. It's just that... well, I was sort of looking forward to trying to get this place organized."

"You can still do that, Bee," Junebug sez, winkin' at him. "We still need to know what's going on, even if we only use the information to slow things up."

"It's just too bad we don't have our own teamsters," Shu Flie sez. "Then we could *really* mess things up."

"What was that, Shu?" Nunzio sez, suddenly lookin' real attentive.

"What? Oh. Well, I was thinking that if we could have our own drivers to do the delivering instead of using army wagons, we could scatter our shipments all across the kingdom."

"No... I mean what did you say about teamsters?"

"Teamsters," Shu repeats. "You know. The guys that drive freight wagons... at least, that's what we called 'em back on the farm."

I look at Nunzio and he looks at me, and I realize from our smiles we is thinkin' the same thing.

"Spyder," I sez, "you found the Mob once in Twixt... do you think you could do it again?"

"Sure," she shrugs. "Why?"

"I got a message I want you to get to Don Bruce," I smiles. "I think we just found somethin' he can do to help us."

Chapter 17

"Ya gotta speak the language."
N. Webster

Hey, Swatter," Shu Flie sez, lookin' out one of the warehouse windows, "do you know there are a buncha wagons and drivers sitting outside?"

"No," I sez, "but if you hum a couple bars, I'll fake it."

Okay, so it's an old joke. Like I've said before, the army runs on old jokes. Unfortuitously, this particular joke is apparently a little *too* old for our farm-raised colleague.

"Say what?" he sez, lookin' kinda puzzled.

"Strike that," I sez. "Are they army or civilian?"

While it is procedure to have army wagons and drivers take shipments out of the supply depot, deliveries from suppliers is done by the

supplier's own transports, and are therefore civilian.

"Civilian," Shu sez.

"Are the wagons full or empty?"

"They look empty from here."

I look over at Nunzio.

"Think it might be the teamsters we're expectin'?"

"Easy enough to check," he shrugs. "Hey
Shu! What are they doing?"

"Nothing," the Flie brother reports. "They're
just sitting around and talking."

"Sounds like them," Nunzio smirks. "I
think it's your deal, Junebug."

As you might be able to detect from this
last comment, we're all occupied with our favorite pastime, which is to say, Dragon Poker.

"Shouldn't one of you go out and talk to
them or something?" Shu sez, wanderin' over to
our table.

"It wouldn't do any good," I sez, peekin' at
my hole cards. "They'll talk to us when they're
good and ready... and not before. Pull up a
chair and relax."

As it turns out, it is several hours before
there is any contact with the drivers. When it
finally comes, it takes the form of a big, potbel-
lied individual with a tattoo on his arm who
comes waddlin' through the door and over to
our game.

"Hey, **hey**!" he snarls, "is somebody gonna
talk to us or what?"

Now, just because Nunzio and me is big
guys what get our way by tossin' our weight
around does not mean we are particularly tol-
erant of anyone else who does the same thing.

"We figured you guys would talk to us

when you were good and ready and not before," Nunzio sez, gettin' to his feet. *"You got a problem with that?"*

"Oh yeah?" the guy hollers, goin' nose to nose with Nunzio. *"Well for your information, we'll talk when we're good and...* and... oh. Yeah."

It takes a little doin', but I manage to hide my smile. This guy is already at a disadvantage in the negotiations, as my cousin has beaten him to his own punch line. Havin' lost the edge in the bluster department, he retreats to his secondary defense of indifference.

"We... ah... heard around that you guys was lookin' for some civilian transport, so we thought we'd drop by and see what the score was for ourselves."

"The stuff's over there on the loadin' dock," I sez, jerkin' a thumb in the appropriate direction. "And here's the list of where it's supposed to go. Bill us."

I nod to Bee, who hands the guy the papers for the shipments we have selected. Like I say, we'd been expecting them.

The guy looks at the list he's holdin' like it's a road kill.

"Just like that, huh?" he sneers. "Don't you wanna talk about our haulin' rates?"

"No need for that," I shrugs. "I'm sure you'll charge us a fair price."

"You are?" he sez, squintin' suspicious-like.

"Sure," I sez, givin' him my best collection agent's smile, "especially seein' as how the rates is gonna be reviewed... and if they look outta line, there's gonna be an investigation."

"An investigation," the driver sneers. "We get Royal investigations all the time... and we ain't changed nothin' yet. If they give us too much grief, we just threaten to shut down haulin' all over the kingdom."

"We wasn't talkin' about a Royal Investigation," Nunzio sez. "We was thinkin' of another judgmental body."

"Oh yeah? Like who?"

Nunzio winks at me, and I take a deep breath and give it my best shot.

"Don... de don don. Don... de don don Bruuuuuce!"

Though my singin' voice is not what you would call a real show stopper, the guy gets the message. His smile droops, and he swallows hard... but he's a fighter and tries to rally back.

"Yeah, okay, so you get our 'special' rates. Just don't expect any express delivery."

Now it's Nunzio's turn to show off his grin.

"Friend," he sez, "if we wanted efficiency, we wouldn't have sent for the teamsters."

"What's that supposed to mean?" the guy bellows, gettin' back some of the color he lost when we mentioned Don Bruce.

"Just that your normal delivery schedules will suit us fine," I sez, innocent-like. "Know what I mean?"

"Yeah... well... I guess that's settled," the guy sez, lookin' back and forth between Nunzio and the men. "We'll go ahead and get started."

As he is goin', I find I cannot resist takin' one last dig at him.

"Say, Nunzio," I sez in a loud voice. "What do you call a teamster in a three piece suit?"

"The defendant!" Nunzio shoots back just as loud.

This humor goes right past the others in the crew, but the driver gets it. He breaks stride, and for a second I think he's gonna come back to "discuss" it with us at length. Instead, he just keeps on goin' and contents himself with slammin' the door for his witty response.

"You know, Guido," Nunzio sez, goin' back to studyin' his cards, "special rates or not, eventually we're going to have to pay these jokers... and we do not currently have access to the funds we are accustomed to operating with in M.Y.T.H. Inc."

"Relax, cuz," I sez, seein' the current bet and raisin' it, "I got an idea for that, too."

*

I have a chance to try out my plan that afternoon when a shipment arrives from one of our suppliers. I wait until the unloadin' is almost complete, then amble over to the driver.

"Say... you got a minute?" I sez, friendly like.

"Okay," the driver shrugs. "What's up?"

"Well," I sez, lookin' around like I'm expectin' a cop, "I got some information you should pass back to your outfit."

"What's that?"

"There's a rumor goin' around that the queen is callin' for an audit on military spendin'," I sez. "somethin' about a lot of our suppliers chargin' us more for supplies than they do civilians."

"An audit?" he repeats, suddenly lookin' real nervous.

"Yeah, scuttlebutt has it that any outfit caught gougin' extra profits out of army contracts is gonna get shut down and their entire inventory confiscated by the government."

"Is that legal?"

"Hey, we're talkin' the queen here. If she sez it's legal, it's legal."

"When is this gonna happen?"

"Not until next month, the way I hear it," I sez. "I just thought you might like to know a little in advance. You know, so just in case any of youse guys' prices should need some quick readjustin', youse could do it *before* the audit started."

"Hey thanks! I appreciate that."

"Yeah? Well, let your management know about it and see if they appreciate it, too. If they do, then maybe it would be a good think if in addition to adjustin' their prices, they made a little *refund* to postdate the price change... like maybe you could drop it off here when you make your next delivery?"

'I'll do that," he sez, noddin' vigorously. "And thanks again. We won't forget you."

*

Things went pretty smooth after that. We only had to plant our audit rumor a couple times for the word to spread through the suppliers, and soon there was a steady arrival of "refunds"... more than enough to pay off the teamsters. What's more, Bee's plan for reorganizin' the warehouse worked well enough that we ended up havin' a fair amount of leisure time each day, which we devoted to sharpenin' our Dragon Poker skills... as well as to our new hobby: Creative Supplyin'.

This pastime proved to be a lot more fun than any of us had anticipated, mostly because of the rules we set for ourselves. Since we agreed to only botch up one out of every ten orders, we have a lot of time to decide exactly which orders will get botched up and how. You see, to keep ourselves covered, we decide that it is best to switch items that either had identification numbers close enough to each other that the error would seem like a simple mis-readin', like a 6 for an 8... or that were of a similar nature or appearance so it would just look like we pulled the wrong item, like sendin' summer weight uniforms to an outfit requestin' winter weight gear.

My personal favorite was when we sent several cases of Propaganda Leaflets to an outfit that was desperately askin' for toilet paper. It seemed somehow appropriate to me.

Like I say, it was a lot of fun... so much fun, in fact, I had a sneaky feelin' that it couldn't last. As it turned out, I was right.

The end of the festivities came when I got an order to report to our commandin' officer.

*

"Stand easy, Sergeant Guido. I've just been reviewing your unit's efficiency rating, and from what I'm seeing, it looks like it's time we had a talk."

I am more puzzled than nervous at this, as we have not been forwardin' the required copies of our paperwork... mostly because we have not been fillin' out the required paperwork at all. This is confirmed by the officer's next words.

"It seems your squad is not overly fond of filling out the supply forms required by regulations, sergeant."

"Well, sir, we've been pretty busy tryin' to learn the routine. I guess we've gotten a little behind in our reports."

"'A little behind' hardly describes it," he sez, tightenin' his lips a little. "I can't seem to find a single form from your supply depot since took over. No matter, though. Fortunately there is sufficient cross-reporting to give me an idea of your progress."

This makes me a little uneasy, as we have figured there would be several rounds of requests and admonishments on our negligent paperwork performance before any attention was paid to the actual performance of our jobs. Still, as I am not totally unaccustomed to havin' to explain my actions to assorted authority figures, I have my alibis ready to go.

"Are you aware, sergeant, that your squad is performing at ninety-five percent efficiency?"

"Ninety-five percent?" I sez, genuinely surprised, as our one-in-ten plan should be yieldin' an even ninety percent.

"I know it sounds high," the officer sez, misunderstandin' my reaction, "especially considering that sixty-five percent is the normal efficiency rating, even for an experienced supply crew. Of course, a practiced eye can read between the lines and get a pretty good idea of what's happening."

"Sir?"

"Take this one shipment, for example," he sez, tappin' one of the sheets in front of him. "It took a shrewd eye with attention to detail to spot that this request for winter weight uniforms was actually several months old, and to realize that substituting summer weight uniforms would be more appropriate."

A small alarm started goin' off in the back of my head, but the officer was still talkin'.

"...or take this item, when you substituted cases of these propaganda leaflets for toilet paper. Everybody's heard about the morale problem of that unit, but it seems you not only had

202

an idea about what to do, you acted on it. It's worked, incidentally... word is, their *esprit de corps* is at an all-time high since receiving your shipment."

As he is speakin' I am starin' at the leaflet he has shoved across the desk. Now understand, we had sent this stuff out without openin' the cartons, so this is the first time I am seein' one of the actual leaflets. It features a large picture of Queen Hemlock, who is not a bad lookin' broad normally, but looks particularly good in this picture as she is wearin' little more than a suggestive smile. Underneath the picture in large letters is the question: WOULDN'T YOU RATHER BY ON *MY* SIDE?" Though I do not pretend to be a sociology expert like my cousin Nunzio, I can see where this would perk up a depressed soldier.

"...But I'm getting bogged down in details," the officer is sayin'.

"In addition to your shipping efficiency, are you aware that the turnaround time for an order at your depot is less than a third the time it takes to get an order through any other depot?"

I am startin' to see the direction this interview is goin', and needless to say I am not enthused with it.

"That's mostly Private Bee's doin' sir," I sez, tryin' to get the focus off me. "He's been experimentin' with a new organization system in our warehouse... as well as a new 'reduced paperwork' trackin' system."

"Private Bee, eh?" the officer sez, makin' a note on his pad. "Tell him I'd like to see him when you get back to your unit. I'd like a bit more information about this experimental system of his... and speaking of experiments..."

He looks up at me again.

"I understand you've been using civilian transports for some of your deliveries. Is that another experiment?"

"Yes, sir," I sez.

I figure he'll be upset about this, so I am willin' to take the blame. It seems, however, that once again I have misjudged the situational.

"You know, sergeant," he sez, leanin' back in his chair, "the army considered using civilian transports for the disbursement of supplies, but abandoned the idea as being too expensive. From the look of things, though, you may have just proved them wrong. Of course, you should have cleared it with me before implementing such an experiment, just as it was beyond your authority to authorize Private Bee to change established procedure, but it's hard to argue with your results. Besides, it's a rare thing these days to find a soldier, especially an enlisted man, who's not afraid to show a little initiative."

I experience a sinkin' feelin' in my stomach.

"...And if there's one thing an organization that's growing as fast as ours needs..."

I close my eyes.

"...it's *leadership*. That's why it gives me such great pleasure to approve your promotion to lieutenant, and..."

My eyes snap open.

"Wait a minute!" I sez, forgettin' all about the proper modes of addressin' a superior. *"You're makin' me an officer??"*

My reaction seems to take the officer by surprise.

"Well... yes," he sez. "Normally we'd require your attending officers' school, but in this situation..."

"That does it!!" I snarl, losin' my temper completely. *"I QUIT!!"*

Chapter 18

"Has anybody got a plan?"
G.A. Custer

To say the least, our reunion with the rest of the M.Y.T.H. Inc. team at Big Julie's was somethin' less than a celebration.

Oh, we are all glad to see each other, and our host is more than generous with the wine from his vineyard, but contrary to popular belief, drinkin' does not necessarily improve one's mood. To my experience, what it does is to *amplify* whatever mood youse is already in... so if youse is happy, youse gets *very* happy, and if youse happens to be depressed, youse gets *very* depressed... and the unfortuitous circumstantial was that we was not very happy.

There is no gettin' around the fact that we have failed dismally in our efforts to stop Queen Hemlock, and while we could try to convince ourselves that it was an impossible task for five individuals and a dragon to achieve, this is the first time since we incorporated that we have failed to come through on an assignment. Realizin' that it wasn't a *real* job, as in one we had been commissioned for, but just a favor for the Boss didn't help much... as, if anythin', we felt worse about lettin' the Boss down than we would about refundin' a client's fee.

"Did you have much trouble getting out of your enlistment?" Tananda was sayin' after we finish explainin' why we are back.

"Not really," Nunzio sez, refillin' his goblet from a pitcher of Big Julie's wine. "Oh, eventually we had to call in General Badaxe to approve it, but after we told him we were on a special assignment for Skeeve, he signed the papers without asking any more questions. The only problem we had was that they *really* wanted us to stay... right, *Lieutenant?*"

He starts to grin at me, then notices from the look on my face that I am not in a mood to be kidded.

"Fortunately," he continues hastily, "the bait they kept offering was to promote us even higher... which, to say the least, was a temptation we had no difficulty resisting."

What my cousin is carefully omittin' from his report is that the *real* problem we had with leavin' wasn't with the army... it was with our crew. Speakin' for myself, I hadn't realized how much they all meant to me until our discharges had been approved and we was ready to say goodbye. I guess it wasn't until then that it hit me that I'd probably never see any of them again.

"Goodbye, Guido," Spellin' Bee had said, shakin' my hand solemnly. "I really appreciate the help you've given me with my magik. I guess I've been so caught up learning the techniques that I've never stopped to think of all the ways it can actually be applied."

"That's nothin'," I sez, feelin' a little embarrassed. "When you get out, look us up and I'll introduce you to the Boss. He knows a lot more about that magik stuff than I do, and I don't think he'll mind givin' you a few pointers."

"Do you really think that would be all right?" Bee sez. "I haven't said anything before, but the Great Skeeve has always been sort of an idol to me. I... I'm not sure I can learn enough about magik here in the army to where he'd want to bother with me."

"There's magik and there's magik," Nunzio sez, puttin' a hand on Bee's shoulder. "I think he'd like to meet you even if you don't get any more magik training than you've got right now. That was a pretty impressive system you came up with for organizing the warehouse, and our outfit is always on the lookout for... ah, *administrators*."

I roll my eyes and he shrugs at me, apologetic-like.

The commandin' officer had been impressed with Bee's system... so much, in fact, that he was bein' promoted and transferred into the task force assigned to improving' the army's efficiency. Consequently, there was some question in the minds of Nunzio and me if he would ever actually see any further magik trainin'... which was, I guess, why Nunzio said what he did.

Personally, I wasn't sure we could use Bee

if he *did* show up, as the M.Y.T.H. Inc. operation is service-oriented and therefore doesn't have any warehouses, but I kept this thought to myself.

"Gee, thanks guys," Bee sez, blinkin' a bit more than usual. "Well... see you around, I guess."

"You guys take care of yourselves... you hear?" Spyder sez, standin' on her tiptoes to give each of us a big hug.

"Sure, Spyder," I sez, blinkin' a little myself. "And listen... when you get out... if you're still interested in joinin' the Mob, you come see us first... got that?"

"Got it," she sez, noddin' vigorous-like.

"...and stay away from Snake," Nunzio sez, "you want help... you come to *us!*"

"Sure thing... and you guys remember, if you need any help... well, if there's anything you think I can help you with, you let me know and I'll be there. Okay?"

"That goes for the rest of us too, Swatter," Shu Flie sez, grabbin' my hand and pumpin' it once. "You give the word, and we'll come runnin'."

"I'll remember," I sez. "Just let us know when you all get out. We wouldn't want to interfere with your army duties."

I meant is as a kind of a joke, but they all seemed to take it serious.

"Don't worry about that," Junebug sez, lookin' me in the eye hard-like. "We know where our first loyalties lie... and you do, too."

Like I said, it wasn't an easy partin'. The hardest part, though, was knowin' that whatever we said about them lookin' us up, the odds were that if they did try, they probably wouldn't be able to find us. As soon as this assignment is over, we'll be headin' back to our headquarters at the Bazaar, and unless they learn how to dimension-travel...

"So what do we do now?" Tananda sez, pullin' my mind away from my memories and bringin' it back to the present. "Pack it up and head for home?"

"I believe there *is* one more option which I brought up at the beginning of this assignment," Massha sez slowly, starin' into her wine.

It takes me a second to remember, but finally it comes back to me.

"You mean, whackin' the queen?" I sez.

She nods. Then there is a long time when no one sez anything as each of us thinks it through.

"Well," Nunzio sez finally, "I suppose we should give it a shot... at least then we can say we tried *everything* before we gave up."

I hesitate a second longer, then nod my agreement.

"All right, cuz," I sez, "you're on. Big Julie, if you can find that gear we stored here before we enlisted, Nunzio and me can..."

"Whoa... stop... HOLD IT!!" Massha sez, holdin' up a hand. "Who said you two were going to be the ones to go after the queen?"

"Well... it's oblivious, ain't it?" I sez, a little annoyed that my attempt to grab the assignment has been thwarted, but willin' to try to bluff my way through. "I mean, this is right up our alley... seein's as how it is what we are trained to do."

"...And from what you've said about your disagreements with your drill instructor, that training is geared more toward enforcing than

210

killing."

"Don't you worry about that," Nunzio sez, givin' her a tight little smile. "We're just against *unnecessary* killing. In this case, it seems that it's necessary."

"Well, when I suggested it, I figured that *I* was going to be the one to go after her," Massha sez, with no trace of her normal 'happy-fat-lady-vamp act.'

"You?" I sez. "Excuse me for pointin' it out, Massha, but though you're more than a little intimidatin' physically, I don't think that physical acts are your forte."

"Who said anything about getting physical?" she sez, holdin' up her ring-laden hands. "You think I wear all this stuff for decoration... or ballast? I've got a few toys here that should take care of things just fine."

Although she is still a beginner in the *natural* magik department, Massha held her own as a city magician for a long time before she signed on as the Boss's apprentice on the strength of the *mechanical* magikal gear she has collected... most of which is in the form of jewelry. While I have suspected as much ever since we first met, this is the first time that she has confirmed that at least some of her baubles are of a lethal variety.

"Besides," she finishes, crossin' her arms decisively, "I'm Skeeve's apprentice... so the job falls to me."

"...And *we're* his bodyguards who are specifically supposed to eliminate any threats to the Boss's well being," Nunzio snaps back. "While I don't doubt your sincerity *or* the reliability of your toys, Massha, whackin' somebody takes *experience*... and Guido and I are the only ones on the team with experience in that area."

"Aren't you forgetting something, boys?" Tananda purrs, breakin' into the argument.

"What's that, Tananda?"

"While you two may be trained and experienced as *generalists* in controlled violence, part of *my* background is specifically as an assassin. By your own logic, then, it looks like the unpleasant task falls to *me*."

"Not to spoil your fun, little sister," Chumley sez, "but I was rather counting on giving it a go myself."

'You?" Tananda laughs. "Come on, big brother, you've still got your arm in a sling."

"What... this?" the troll sez, glancin' down at this arm. "It's hardly worth mentioning, really."

He pulls his arm out of the sling and wiggles his fingers, then sets his elbow on the table beside him.

"Do any of you want to try arm wrestling with me? Or will you concede the point?"

"Really, Chumley," Tananda sez, ignorin' the challenge, "just because that thick hide of yours is hard to get through..."

"...Is the exact reason why *I'm* the logical choice for the assignment," the troll finishes with a smile.

"...Except for the minor detail of your appearance," Massha adds. "Sorry, Chumley, but you're the last of us I'd figure for the assignment. Any of the rest of us could pass for natives, but you'd stand out like a sore thumb without a disguise spell."

"So I borrow little sister's makeup mirror."

"Not a chance," Tananda sez, stubbornlike.

212

"...Or I simply borrow a hooded cloak or something for a disguise," Chumley continues smoothly as if she hasn't spoken. "How about it, Big Julie? Have you got anything lying around in an extra-extra large?"

"As a matter of fact," the retired general sez, "I was thinking of doing the job myself."

"What?"

"You?"

"That's..."

"...BECAUSE," Big Julie continues, silencing us all with the simple technique of raisin' that voice of his to an authoritative level, "because I'm an old man and therefore the most expendable."

We all sink back into our chairs, too embarrassed to look at each other. With these few words, he has gotten to the heart of what was prompting our apparently bloodthirsty argument.

"I've been listening to all of you," he sez, takin' advantage of our uneasy silence, "and what nobody seems to want to say out loud is that trying the assassinate the queen is pretty much a suicide mission. Political leaders... and particularly royalty... are the best guarded folks in any nation. Even if you can get to them, which is uncertain at best, the odds of getting away afterward are so small they aren't even worth considering."

He looks around the gatherin'.

"Of course, I don't have to tell you this because you all know it already. That's why each of you is so eager to take the job... to let the others off the hook by nobly sacrificing yourself. Well, my advice, as your tactical advisor, is to forget the whole thing and go home...

since I don't believe Skeeve ever intended for things to go this far... or, if you're determined to have the queen killed, then to let me do it. Like I said before, I'm an old man who's doing nothing but idling away my retirement with petty self-indulgences. All of you are contributing more to life, and are therefore more valuable, than I am. Besides," he lets a little grin play across his face, "it might be kinda fun to see a little action just one more time. I never really figured on dying in bed."

"That's sweet of you, Big Julie," Tananda sez, "but it's totally out of the question. Even though you've worked with us as an advisor, you're not really part of the team... and I'm *sure* this is one job Skeeve wouldn't want us to subcontract."

"I think we're agreed at least on that," Massha sez, glancin' around our assemblage. "If it's going to be done, it's going to be done by one of us."

"Then you still figure to try for Hemlock?" the ex-general frowns.

"I think," Chumley announces, standin' up and stretchin', "I think that we're all too tired and have been drinking far too much to make a rational decision. I suggest we all retire for now and pick up this discussion in the morning when our heads are clearer."

"You know, that's the first sensible idea I've heard in the last half hour," Tananda sez, stretchin' a bit herself... which would be fun to watch if I wasn't still thinkin' about the problem at hand.

"Good thinking, Chumley," Nunzio sez.

"Right."

"Sounds good to me."

214

With everyone in agreement, the party breaks up and we all start to drift off to our rooms.

"Nunzio," I sez, as soon as the others are out of hearin' range. "Are you thinkin' what I'm thinkin'?"

"That we should figure on getting up a little early tomorrow?" he sez.

"...Because if anyone goes for the queen, it's gonna be us." I declare.

"...And if we leave it to the group to decide, someone else might get the job..." he adds.

"...Whereas if we simply present them with a *fait accompli*, it'll be too late to argue," I finish. "Right?"

"Right," he answers.

Like I say, though Nunzio and I sometimes have our differences, we work together pretty well when the stakes are high... which is why we are both smilin' as we wave good night to the others.

Chapter 19

"We must hurry... it's almost over!"
P. Fogg

As I mentioned, Nunzio and me have brought along a few accessories on this assignment which we stored at Big Julie's for fear the army might be less than appreciative if we showed up to enlist already equipped... especially as our personal gear tends to be of a much better quality than that which the army issues.

Bein' true professionals, we spend considerable time sortin' through our travelin' kits for items which would be of specific use for the job at hand. The knuckle dusters, sawed-off pool cues, lead pipes and such we set aside... as they would normally be used for much more subtle ventures, and attemptin' to apply them in a fatal manner would be both time-consumin' and messy. Though it broke our hearts, we also decide to leave behind our Iolo cross-bows. While they are great in an open confrontation, they are a bit bulky to be considered as concealable weapons which counts against them as whatever we use will have to be carried in under the noses of the queen's guards. While these deletions shorten our equipment list somewhat, we are still left with a fair assortment of tools from which to make our final selection.

Nunzio finally settles on a pocket, pistol-grip crossbow and a length of piano wire... just in case... while I opt for a blowgun and a nice set of throwin' knives. For those of youse who may be surprised by the latter choice, I would note that while I might not be as good as Snake is, I am still no slouch when it comes to shivs. Unfortunately I cannot provide youse with references to this fact, as those who would be in a position to testify on the degree of my skill from firsthand experience are, unfortuitously, no longer with us... but I digress.

"You know, Guido," Nunzio sez, startin' to stash his gear in the spiffy civilian clothes we're now wearin' again, "there *is* one problem with us taking this contract on ourselves."

"What's that?"

"Well, if we get caught afterwards, which as Big Julie points out is a definite possibility if not a probability, then we are again faced with a situation where it looks like the Mob is interfering with the kingdom of Possiltum.

"Come on, Nunzio," I sez. "We have been workin' for the Mob for a number of years now, and in all that the time the authorities have not even come close to provin' there is any direct

217

connection between ourselves and that august organization."

"I wasn't thinking about the authorities," my cousin sez, grim like. "I was thinking about Don Ho and the other Mob bosses to which Don Bruce referred."

"Oh... Yeah."

I had not considered this, but it is definitely a point worth reflectin' upon. However, I am still unwillin' to let one of the others on the M.Y.T.H. Inc. team take the fall instead of us.

"Tell you what," I sez. "Chances are, only one of us will do the actual whackin'... right?"

"Well, yeah. So?"

"So if it looks like he's gonna get caught, then the other one whacks *him*. Then the survivor can say that the one what whacked the queen was a renegade, and was eliminated for violatin' the Boss's orders."

"Sounds good to me," Nunzio sez. "Let's get going."

If, perhaps, our attitude toward dyin', not to mention the possibility of maybe whackin' each other, sounds a little callous, I would suggest youse consider anew what it is Nunzio and me do for a livin'. We is bodyguards... which means that along with our jobs, we accept the possibility that at some point one or both of us might have to die so that the person what we are protectin' does not. I repeat, it is part of the job... and we'd be pretty dumb bunnies if that part of the job description came as a surprise to us after all this time.

As to the possibility of one of us havin' to whack the other... well, I don't relish the thought of droppin' Nunzio any more than I like the idea of him droppin' me. Still, once one has

218

accepted the above referenced possibility of dyin' on the job to protect the Boss's body or reputation, then it requires little additional justification to accept that dead is dead and afterwards it doesn't really matter exactly who it was what did the number on youse. If anythin', if Nunzio did me or vice versa, then at least we would be assured of it bein' a neat, professional job with a minimum of fuss and bother.

Anyhow, it is just after dawn as we sneak out of the villa, openin' the door an inch at a time in case it squeaks, then easin' onto the patio as soon as it's open far enough for us to slip through. At this point, seein' as how it seems we have effected our exit without arousin' the others on the team, I pause to give Nunzio a wink and a thumbs up sign.

"Morning, boys!" comes a familiar voice from the far side of the patio. "Care for a bit of breakfast?"

Big Julie is sprawled on a recliner, soakin' up the morning sun as he picks at the food laid out on the table next to him.

"Shhh! Could you keep it down?" Nunzio hisses, puttin' a finger to his lips as he hurries over to our host.

"What for?" Big Julie sez, still speakin' in that loud, projectin' voice of his.

"Well... ummm..." I sez, shootin' a glance at Nunzio who just shrugs. "To tell you the truth, Big Julie, we are takin' it on ourselves to bring yesterday's argument to a close by goin' after the queen before there is any further discussion. This effort will, of course, go to waste if the others hear you and emerge before we have made our departure."

"Oh... it's too late to worry about that," he

219

sez, casual like.

"Excuse me?"

"They've already gone... one at a time, of course."

"They did?" When?"

"Well, let's see... Tananda was the first... she left last night... then Chumley took off when he woke up and realized she was gone. Massha... well, she lit out about an hour ago when she found out the others had gone... you know, that woman moves pretty fast considering the weight she's carrying."

"So they're all ahead of us." Nunzio sez, disgusted like. "And here we thought we were being clever getting an early start."

"Well, there *is* one detail I notice your teammates neglected to mention yesterday," Big Julie sez. "You see, today is the day the queen holds her public court and hears cases and complaints from anybody... first come first served. That makes it perfect for the kind of questionable deed you were discussing... but the lines form early, both for those seeking an audience and those who simply want to be *in* the audience."

"Oh that's just swell!" I sez. "Tell me, Big Julie, if you don't mind my askin', why didn't you try to stop them?"

"Me?" he blinks, innocent-like. "I had my say yesterday... and as I recall was unanimously told to butt out. That makes it none of my business... though I'll admit I'd be no more eager to try stopping any of the others than I'd be to try to stop you two. Know what I mean?"

"Yeah, I guess I see your point," Nunzio sez quick-like, lookin' grimmer than I've seen him in a long time. "Well, come on, Guido! We've

220

gotta hurry if we're gonna be in this game at all!"

Just as Big Julie predicted, the palace throne room was packed to the walls with even more folks waiting outside to get in if anyone left early. As I have mentioned before, however, Nunzio and me is of sufficient size that most folks give ground when we crowd them, so we are able to eventually elbow our way in to where we can at least see.

The crowd what has shown up just to watch is linin' the walls about twenty deep or jammed into the balconies, leavin' the center of the room open for those havin' business with the queen. Seein' as how that pack is standin' in a line which stretches back out the door, we have little choice but to join the audience... which hides our presence to a certain extent, but greatly reduces our chances of a quick withdrawal after we finishes workin'.

"There's Massha," I sez, though it's kinda needless, as she is standin' in the line waitin' to go before the queen and is *very* noticeable in that company. "Can you see the others?"

Nunzio just shakes his head and keeps scannin' the audience on our right, so I start doin' the same for the crowd on the left.

Of course, I realize it is unlikely I will be able to spot Tananda, since with that disguise mirror of her she can look like anyone she wants. I suspect though, knowin' her to be more than a little vain, that even disguised she will be both female and attractive.

Chumley, however, is another matter entirely. All I gotta do is look for a good sized figure in an outfit that hides it's face, and...

Nunzio gives me a quick elbow in the ribs to get my attention, then jerks his head up toward the ceilin'. It takes me a minute to figure out what he's tryin' to point out to me, but then somethin' moves in the shadows of the rafters and I see her. It's Tananda, and she's flat on one of the heavy timbers easin' her way closer to the throne. At first, I'm afraid she'll fall, but then I realize that she's...

"Quit looking at her," Nunzio hisses in my ear. "Do you want the guards to spot her?"

I realize I have been starin' up at her like some kind of a tourist, and that if I keep doin' it, other people... like the guards... are gonna start wondering what I'm lookin' at and start checkin' the rafters themselves.

"So what do we do now?" I whispers back, tearin' my eyes away from Tananda's progress.

"We move," Nunzio sez, "...And fast, if we're gonna score before she makes her try. With this crowd, though... tell you what. You try easin' up on the left there and I'll go up this side."

"Got it!" I sez, and put a gentle elbow into the kidney of the guy ahead of me, thereby openin' up a route to the other side of the throne room.

Sayin' we'll get close to the throne, however, proves to be considerably easier than actually gettin' there. At first I am worried about movin' too fast and catchin' the guards' eyes as someone tryin' too hard to get close to where the queen will be. After a few minutes of fightin' with the crowd, though, I am more concerned with bein' able to move at all. It seems like the closer to the front of the room I gets, the more determined the people are to *not* give up their place.

By the time I am halfway to the throne, I am startin' to get desperate over how long it's takin' and look around to see where Nunzio is. As it turns out, he is havin' even more trouble than me, havin' progressed a mere six steps before gettin' boxed in behind a gaggle of old biddies. They are not about to give ground for anyone, and it appears that short of punchin' his way through them, he isn't gonna make it to the front at all.

Of course, this leaves it to me to beat the others to the queen... which suits me just fine. Redoublin' my efforts, I sneak a peek upward to check Tananda's progress, only to find I can no longer see her at all.

Just then, someone lets loose with a blast of brass horns... and the queen appears.

For a moment, I am too stunned to keep pushin' forward... in fact, I lose a couple steps.

You see, I met Queen Hemlock back at the same time I met the Boss, and more recently had a chance to refresh my memory while gazin' at a propaganda leaflet. While she is not what you would call a knockout, neither is she exactly plain. The woman easin' herself onto the throne, however looks so much different than those images that if they hadn't hollered out her name as she walked in, I probably wouldn't have recognized her. Of course, even just passin' her on the street, the crown would have been a pretty strong clue.

She looks like she hasn't been sleepin' very well, as there are big dark circles under her eyes, and it looks like she's been off her feed... well, more so than normal as she's always been a bit on the scrawny side. Then the first guy in line starts yammerin' about how he thinks his business is payin' too much taxes, and for a minute I think she's gonna burst into tears.

It occurs to me that however successful her expansion program may look from the outside, it doesn't look like it's makin' Queen Hemlock any too happy.

Just then I spot Chumley... or at least a big figure in a hooded cloak... edgin' along the wall behind the guards not ten feet from where the queen is sittin', and know I have run out of time. Slidin' one of the throwin' knives down my sleeve, I start eyeballin' the distance between me and Hemlock. It's gonna be one heck of a throw, but it won't get any easier by my starin' at it, so I step back for balance and...

...And all hell breaks loose at the back of the room!

At first I think the guards have jumped Nunzio, but when I look his way he is standin' clear of the action, lookin' right back at me and pointin' desperately out the door, mouthin' somethin' I can't make out over the hubbub. I crane my neck tryin' to figure out what he's pointin' at, but all I can see is the crowd outside the throne room is partin'... makin' way for something or somebody.

There's a ripple of noise spreadin' forward from the back of the crowd, buildin' in volume as more and more voices join in. Abandonin' my efforts to see what's goin' on, I bend an ear to try to sort out what it is they're sayin'.

"...magician..."

"He's back!"

"HE'S COMING!"

"...COURT MAGICIAN!!!"

"LOOK!! THERE HE IS!! IT'S..."

"THE GREAT SKEEVE!!!"

...And it was!!

Just as I make out the words, the crowd at the back of the throne room parts, and the Boss comes walkin' in... and Aahz is with him!! They seem to be arguin', of course, and are totally ignorin' the crowd around them which first surges back, then presses forward like a wall.

I am out of the audience before I am aware that I have trampled several of Possiltum's citizens in my haste, and pass Massha who is always a little slow off the line because of her size. I see Nunzio comin' through the crowd, knockin' people down like duckpins, and am vaguely aware that I am doin' the same... but I don't care. I am just happy to see the Boss here and in one piece.

"SKEEVE!!"

I hear someone shout in a voice that sorta sounds like the queen's, but by now I am six steps out and closin' fast.

Now, I have never been fond of the Mob tradition of men huggin' each other, but this time I figure to make an exception.

"BOSS!!" I hollers, and throw my arms wide and...

...And the room spins... then everythin' goes black!

Chapter 20

"I want a rematch!"
M. Tyson

Guido! Hey! Come on! Wake up!"

I can hear Nunzio's voice, but decide to keep my eyes closed a little while longer. Havin' had numerous similar experiences in the past, I have no difficulty figurin' out what has happened... which is to say I have been knocked cold. The difficult part is recallin' the circumstantials which led to this condition, a task which is not made any simpler by the fact that my brain is still a little scrambled from the experience... which is why I have chosen to pretend I am still out to lunch whilst I composes myself.

We were in the throne room... then the Boss walked in with Aahz... I started over to greet him... Nunzio was comin' over to do the same thing... then...

I get a fix on Nunzio's location from his voice, then open my eyes and sit up quick-like, grabbin' him by the throat as I do so.

"Did you just sucker punch me, cousin?" I sez, curious-like.

The world starts to spin again a little, makin' me reconsider the wisdom of havin' tried to move so fast so soon after regainin' consciousness, but I blink a couple times to clear my vision and it settles down. I also notice that Nunzio is turnin' a little purple, so I loose my grip on his throat so's he can answer me.

"It... wasn't me!" he squeaks.

Seein' as how Nunzio is usually very proud of his work... particularly on those occasions when he has just worked on me... I figure he is tellin' the truth and open my grip the rest of the way.

"Well if *you* didn't do it," I frowns, still blinkin' a little, "then who..."

"Meet Pookie," he sez, pointin' over my shoulder with his left thumb, as his right hand is busy rubbin' his throat. "She's the Boss's new bodyguard."

"New bodyguard?" I sez, takin' a look behind me and...

The world stops... as does my heart and lungs.

Now, when I say this chick is stunnin', it has nothin' to do with the fact that she just knocked me cold. She has the smooth, strong lines of a panther... except for a few pleasant roundin's one does not normally find on a cat of any size. She also has green scales and yel-

low eyes which are regardin' me levelly.

"Sorry about the mix-up," she sez, not soundin' at all sorry, "but you came in so fast that Skeeve didn't have a chance to tell me you were on our side. Anyway, pleased to meet you... I guess. Here's your knife back."

I look at the throwin' knife she is holdin' out and realize it is indeed one of mine. I musta still been holdin' it in my hand when I went to greet the Boss, which is an embarrassin' oversight. One of the troubles with havin' big hands is that sometimes one forgets one is holdin' things.

"New bodyguard, huh?" I sez, not bein' able to think of anythin' wittier to say as I accepts the knife and stashes it.

"We met on Perv," she sez, a little frosty. "Skeeve needed a bodyguard... and it seems he didn't have one with him."

Now I am not so far gone that I can't spot a professional rebuke when I hear one.

"We didn't like it, either," I growl, "but the Boss *ordered* us not to go along with him and *asked* us to lend a hand here instead."

Pookie thinks about this for a second, then gives a small nod.

"That explains a few things," she sez, unthawin' a little. "Skeeve's being alone had me wondering about you two, but I guess you really didn't have much choice in the matter."

There is no reason why her approval should mean anything to me... but it does.

"So, you're from Perv, huh?" I sez, tryin' to prolong the conversation.

"She's my cousin," Aahz sez, and for the first time I become aware that he is standin' nearby.

In fact, the whole team is standin' here, and I...

"Your cousin!" I sez, the words finally sinkin' in.

"Don't worry," Pookie sez, givin' me a small smile and a wink. "We aren't at all alike."

"Can you guys keep it down?" Tananda hisses at us. "I'm trying to eavesdrop on this!"

Wrenchin' my attention away from Pookie, I finally start to focus in on what's goin' on.

We are still in the throne room, but the crowds are gone. In fact, the whole place... floor and balconies... are empty of people and guards except for us. Well, us and the Boss, who is sittin' on the throne steps chattin' with Queen Hemlock.

"...so everything was going pretty well, until Roddie caught some bug or other and died," she is sayin'. "When I didn't die, too, I realized those rings you gave us didn't *really* link our lives... incidentally, I'd get my money back on those if I were you..."

"You mean the king really *did* die of natural causes?" I whispers.

"So it seems," Tananda murmurs back. "Now put a sock in it. I want to hear this."

"...and you *know* I've always wanted to expand our borders just a teensy tiny bit, so I figured, 'Why not give it a try?'..."

"From what I hear," the Boss interrupts, "the expansion goes way past 'teensy tiny' in anyone's definition."

"I know," the queen sighs, deflatin' a little. "It just seems to have gotten away from me. My advisors... you remember Grimble and Badaxe?... well, they keep assuring me that everything is fine... that as long as I keep lowering the taxes, the people will support me... but I keep having this feeling that I've lost control of..."

"Lowering the taxes while you expand your borders?" the Boss breaks in. "But that can't be done! A bigger kingdom means *more* expense, not *less!* You still have the cost of local government, *plus* the cost of extra layers of bureaucracy to manage the local bureaucracies."

It finally dawns on me what has been botherin' me about this 'lower taxes' thing every time I hear about it. I also remember that I had to take Econ. 101 three times.

"I know," the queen sez. "I've been covering the extra cost from my old kingdom's treasury, but that's almost gone. Grimble keeps saying that things will level off eventually when the kingdom gets big enough, but..."

"It's not going to happen," the Boss sez, shakin' his head. "You can't beat the mathematics of the situation. You're either going to have to raise the taxes or pull your boarders back... or go bankrupt."

"Oh Skeeve!" Hemlock sez, givin' him a quick hug. "I *knew* you could figure it out. That's why I sent for you."

"Sent for me?"

"Of course, silly. The ring. Didn't you get it?"

"Well, yes. But..."

"I never was much good with letters," the queen continues, "but I was *sure* you'd get the message when I sent you Roddie's ring... of course, I had to send a little of *him* along with it... you were right about the rings not coming off, by the way."

"That was *Rodrick's* ring?"

"Of course. You don't think I'd cut off *my* finger, do you?"

She holds up her hand and waggles her fingers at him... all of them, includin' the one with her ring on it. The skin on the finger we had gotten had been so soft and smooth, we had all *assumed* it as a woman's finger. Of course, stoppin' to think about it, kings don't work much with their hands, either.

"Anyway, you got the message, and you're here now... so everything's going to be all right."

"The message," the Boss sez, lookin' a little confused... which to my mind is understandable. "Umm... just to be sure we understand each other, would you mind saying what you wanted to tell me in words instead of using... graphic communications?"

"Isn't it obvious?" the queen sez. "I need your help to manage things, so I'm offering you a position."

"Well... I'm kind of busy these days," the Boss sez, "but I guess I can spare a little time to help you straighten things out as your advisor..."

"...as my *consort*," the queen corrects.

The whole team flinches at this, and we swap a few worried looks back and forth between us.

The Boss, however, is a little slower on the uptake.

"...of course, the first thing you'll have to do is to order the army to stop advancing until we figure out what to do next."

"Consider it done. ...and then Grimble and I will... CONSORT??!!"

As I have said, the Boss can be a bit slow

232

from time to time, but eventually he catches on.

"Of course," Hemlock beams at him. "I figure we can get married, then if we divvy up some of these bothersome duties, we'll still have time to..."

"*CONSORT???*"

The Boss seems to be stuck on the word.

"That's right," the queen says, cocking her head at him. "Why? Have you got a problem with that?"

The temperature in the throne room seems to drop along with the chilly tone in her voice.

"...Because if you do, there *is* another option. I can do what you suggested back when Roddie and I got married."

"Which was...?" The Boss sez in a small voice.

"Abdicate." Somehow the queen manages to make the one word sound like a sentence... a death sentence. "I can step down from the throne and name *you* my successor. Then you can try to run this whole mess all by yourself!"

Check and mate.

This whole conversation is makin' me more than a little uneasy... but that is nothin' compared to what it is doin' to the Boss. He looks absolutely panicky... not to mention sorta green around the gills.

"I... I..." he stammers.

"...But don't you think it'll be so much nicer if you just go along with my original idea?" Hemlock sez, all kittenish again. "That way, you get the whole kingdom *and* me!"

"I... I don't know," the Boss manages at last. "I've never thought about getting married."

"Well think about it," the queen sez, gettin'

a bit of an edge on her voice.

"No... I mean, I'll need some *time* to think about it."

"Okay," Hemlock nods. "That's fair."

"Maybe in a year..."

"...I'll give you a *month*," the queen sez, actin' like the Boss hadn't said anythin'. "Then I'll expect your answer one way or the other. In the meantime, *I'll* order the army to stop and *you* can start going over the books with Grimble. I mean, that will be a good idea whatever decision you make, won't it?"

"I... I guess so."

This is not lookin' good. The Boss has never been good with skirts, and it looks like Hemlock is gonna be able to lead him around by the nose.

"I think I've heard enough," Tananda sez. "I'll see you guys later."

"Where are you going, little sister?" Chumley sez, voicin' the question for all of us. "It looks like Skeeve is going to need all the help we can give him... and then some."

"Actually," she sez, "I was going to head back to the home office. I figure I need a little break, so I thought I'd tend the home fires while my hair grows back."

"Really?" Chumley frowns.

"Of course," she purrs, flashin' a wide smile, "that will free *Bunny* from her duties. I think I'll send her back here to lend a hand."

"Bunny?"

"Well you can't expect Skeeve to straighten things out here without his administrative assistant, can you?" she sez, innocent-like. "Besides, Bunny's a lot better at dealing with figures than I am."

She pauses and sends one last dark look at the queen.

"...at least, I figure in *this* situation she will be."

NEXT: Skeeve tries to unravel the puzzle of the opposite sex in...
Sweet Myth-tery Of Life.

Robert Asprin is a story-teller in the classic sense. He can come up with a story anytime, anywhere, about *anything* his audience cares to read--or hear, since his talents do not limit him to the written word. His books range from the futuristic corporate structures of *The Cold Cash Wars* to the martial intrigue of *Tambu* to the gritty ruthlessness of the *Thieves' World* anthologies as well as the rambling, road-show hilarity of the *Myth Adventure* books.

Of Philippine-Irish descent, Asprin currently resides in Ann Arbor, Michigan. His interests (and abilities) are too numerous to list in their entirety, but include music, weapons, theater arts, tropical fish breeding, and martial arts.

Phil Foglio is a multitalented individual. He's an accomplished artist, writer, cartoonist, satirist, card shark --the list goes on. His cartoons and illustrations have appeared in *Starlog*, *The Dragon*, and *Swank* as well as Starblaze Editions. He is the creator/ artist of the graphic series *D'Arc Tangent* and *Buck Godot*. With Robert

Asprin, Phil Foglio has worked on adapting the *Myth Adventures* novels into a comic format. Foglio resides in Chicago, Illinois.